D1615994

Haycastle's Cricket

Matilda Haycastle is having a bad day. There's a run-away wolf at the bottom of her garden, and her eccentric uncle Edward has just invited himself to stay, together with his house-proud but accident-prone research assistant Byron T. Kaplan.

Gentleman-explorer and discoverer of a new species of cricket, *Gryllulus haycastellani*, Edward is in Brussels to attend a conference on conservation. But clearly that's not all he's here for. Someone is out to kill him; and he's making no secret of his hatred for the conference chairman, Philippe Andrieu, a very powerful Belgian businessman.

Just what is the cause of this bitter resentment? Why does Edward break into Andrieu's car and then lie to the police? And, more importantly, when Andrieu is suddenly found murdered, can it be mere coincidence that Edward has no alibi?

Matilda is convinced her uncle is no killer – but she cannot possibly envisage the shocking secret she is about to uncover, a secret that will rock her to the core . . .

Haycastle's Cricket

Michèle Bailey

MACMILLAN

First published 1996 by Macmillan

an imprint of Macmillan General Books
25 Eccleston Place, London SW1W 9NF
and Basingstoke

Associated companies throughout the world

ISBN 0 333 65618 0

9 8 7 6 5 4 3 2 1

A CIP catalogue record for this book is available from
the British Library

Phototypeset by Intype, London
Printed by Mackays of Chatham PLC, Chatham, Kent

Chapter 1

I remember the day my uncle Edward phoned, because it was the day I found a wolf at the bottom of my garden.

You'll tell me that wolves aren't exactly part of the scenery in the south-eastern suburbs of Brussels, and you'd be right. I should have realised something unusual was up when my cat Hortense shot in from the garden with a tail like a flue-brush and disappeared into the cupboard in the upstairs loo. This was uncharacteristic of a cat who is second cousin to Godzilla. I peered out of the kitchen window, and saw a long darkish-grey shape with pricked ears lying under my pear tree. Somebody's young Alsatian, I thought, and set off up the garden to negotiate. But when I was halfway there, it lifted a strange, wild face, and I stopped and went rather suddenly into reverse.

It was undoubtedly a wolf. From the safety of the kitchen window, I saw it drop its muzzle on its front paws with an air of weary relief. It didn't seem to be going anywhere.

Why am I the one who always gets to deal with these things? Resisting the temptation to join Hortense in the upstairs loo, I reviewed the possibilities for action. Call the police? They'd cordon off the street, bring in a squadron of armed helicopters and shoot the poor beast full of holes. The Société Royale Protectrice des Animaux? Excuse me, but there's a wolf at the bottom of my garden. Who was going to believe me?

There wasn't actually much choice, so I dialled the SRPA's number and explained the situation, hoping they wouldn't think I was a complete nutter. But the woman at the SRPA sounded perfectly matter-of-fact. Somebody would come round as soon as possible. Could they have my name and address?

'Matilda Haycastle. I live in Boitsfort.' I gave the address and phone number, and heard scritching at the other end as the information was written down.

'Keep your children and domestic animals inside,' the woman said. 'Is the wolf showing signs of moving off?'

I peered out of the window again, stretching the phone cord. The wolf appeared to be catching up on its beauty sleep.

'It's snoozing,' I said. 'Should I warn my neighbours?'

'Better not risk a panic,' said the SRPA. 'Just keep an eye on it for the time being. We'll be round in a few minutes.'

It was a sunny Tuesday morning and luckily there wasn't anybody about. We were right in that lull after the wage-earners have driven off to the office, before the daytime life of the street begins with young mothers pushing babies down to the local play-area, people going shopping and walking dogs, delivery vans arriving and housewives in cotton overalls getting busy on the day's cleaning.

I wasn't working that week. I hadn't worked the week before either. The recession was beginning to look permanent, and the usual summer rush on temp secretaries was starting late this year. But I can't say I minded too much. The weather had been great so far, and I had my own house and garden to play with, a new and intoxicating experience. And, for the moment, there was money in the bank. A little, anyway.

The wolf seemed to have dug in for the day. I checked my watch. Ten minutes already. That's when the phone rang. I grabbed the whole apparatus and returned to the kitchen window. I heard coins clattering, a confused babble of hollow sounds and voices, and through the crackling on the line, a cheerful voice I hadn't heard for years. 'Matilda? This is Uncle Edward. I'm at Victoria Station.'

One of my uncle Edward's many irritating characteristics is his ability to disappear for years and then ring up and sound as if he last spoke to you yesterday. No hello. No how are you. No explanations or apologies. Hang on. Where did he say he was?

'What are you doing at Victoria Station?' I snapped, the hair rising on the back of my neck at the thought of the possible answer.

The gods weren't smiling today.

'I'm coming to Brussels,' he announced breezily. 'Your mother said you've got a guest room and I wasn't able to get a hotel – it's a conference, last-minute thing – so I wondered if it'd be all right to come to you. It's only for a few days. I shan't get in the way. I'm coming over on the boat and the train gets in at six this evening – Gare du Midi. Can you come down and meet it?'

One of my problems is that I can't think up excuses fast enough. I was still trying to get my mouth into gear when there was a crash and bang at the other end, and my uncle said hurriedly: 'Got to go, they're blowing the whistle. See you tonight. Don't forget, we'll be there at six – Gare du Midi.'

'What do you mean, WE?' I yelled, but the connection was already dead in my hand. I stared at the phone, growling, seized by helpless fury. I hate people inviting themselves. I hate people coming to stay. Now I was going to have to shop, plan meals, make beds up, allow intruders into my new private little world.

3

Never mind growling; I felt like biting someone. And what, horror of horrors, did he mean by WE?

Somebody banged on the front door. My doorbell was lying in bits on the hall floor as I hadn't fixed it yet. I slammed the phone down and went to open. Outside in the sunny street was a large Range Rover with '*Les Fauves asbl*' painted on the side, and one of the most gorgeous men I've ever seen. Tall, lean, serious and dark, with long hair tied at the nape of his neck like an eighteenth-century rake. You've got to have the profile for it – he did. Perhaps the Gods were trying to make up. I rearranged my face into the best approximation of a welcoming smile that I could manage under the circumstances and said: 'You've come about the wolf?' Great conversational opener.

'The SRPA phoned me. Is it still here?' He was carrying something that looked like a case for a musical instrument. He spoke French with the quick, pointed accent of Paris which is so different from broad Belgian French. It was a while since I'd heard it, and I felt a sudden wave of painful nostalgia for the most beautiful city in the world.

'Hasn't budged,' I told him. 'Come in.'

In the kitchen, we stared silently out of the window side by side. He was half a head taller than I, which was unusual but pleasant.

'It's Elizabeth,' he said, half to himself.

'Pardon me?'

He turned his head and glanced at me quickly. Brown eyes, straight black eyebrows, olive skin, meridional-looking. And shy, bless me.

'Her name's Elizabeth. She's from a travelling circus.'

'How did she escape?'

'She didn't. She was let out. The owner was in trouble with the police for ill-treating his animals, and he thought he could avoid prosecution by letting them

4

out during the night, before we came to pick them up.'

'Them?' I asked.

'There were two. Elizabeth and Alexandre.'

'Have you found the other one?'

'Killed on the motorway.' He spoke without emphasis. Turning to the kitchen table, he opened his music case and took out a rifle. As I drew in a breath, he said, with a slight smile: 'Don't worry. It's a dart gun. Tranquillizers.'

He loaded the gun with professional expertise. He was a very unfussy man. Long, tanned hands. No wedding ring.

'You work for the SRPA?' I asked.

'No. I run an animal shelter. Les Fauves.' He looked up with his quick smile. 'I'm new in the job – only been in Brussels a couple of weeks.'

'It's not like Paris, is it?' I said, and he looked startled, then shook his head and laughed.

'How did you know? Are you French?' he asked.

'Half. My mother,' I told him. 'Father's English. But I lived in Paris for a while, in the Rue St Placide.'

'I know it,' he exclaimed. 'My aunt lives there.'

We smiled at each other, pleased as people always are at silly coincidences. His teeth were very white, the canines long and pointed. Very sexy.

He picked up the gun. 'It won't take a minute,' he said reassuringly.

I watched him go up the garden with his long stride. Elizabeth didn't put up any sort of a fight. The animal man waited till the drug had taken effect, then lifted her in his arms, carried her down the garden and through the house, and put her into a large cage in the back of the Range Rover. Then he tramped back in to fetch his gear.

'Is she OK?' I asked.

'Exhaustion, sore feet and years of bad treatment. But she'll be all right now.'

5

'What'll happen to her?'

'We'll try and get her transferred to Italy. There's a wolf reserve down there and she can be released back into the wild. May I wash my hands?'

'Does this kind of thing happen often?' I asked, as he bent over the kitchen sink and turned on the taps.

'Too often. Small travelling circuses are always getting into trouble – there's little or no control in most European countries and it's easy to break rules.'

'And you pick up the pieces?'

'Well, Brussels is a major hub for illegal animal imports – skins, ivory, plants, but also live animals and birds. When any are found, they're sent to us to be looked after till they can be relocated. If they're still alive, that is. But we also take in strays, like any other shelter. Old horses, cats and dogs and so on.' He turned the taps off and straightened up, reaching for the towel which hung by the kitchen window.

I'd read the horror stories in the papers about the crates of dead animals and birds that turn up all too frequently in the cargo holds of major airlines, having starved or suffocated during the long hauls from the Third World. Some of them are lucky – Antwerp Zoo has a whole aviary full of hot macaws. It's a pity they can't talk.

He gave me another of those quick glances, but this time the dense brown eyes remained fixed on mine.

'Maybe you'd like to come and visit the shelter?' he suggested diffidently. 'We're open to visitors, you know. I'll give you the address.'

He reached for the wallet in his back pocket and extracted a card. 'Have you got a pen? I haven't had time to get my own cards printed up,' he said apologetically. I gave him a Bic, and he wrote something on the back of the card and handed it to me. The printing said 'Les Fauves asbl', with 'Philippe Andrieu, Président' underneath that and an address near Ottignies.

6

The handwriting on the back said 'Jean-Loup Perrault, *Directeur*'.

'Jean-Loup!' I exclaimed, laughing at the aptness of it, and he smiled and shrugged, showing those pointed teeth again.

'Surely you didn't come all the way from Ottignies this morning?' I added. 'Not in that time!'

'No, I've got an apartment in Brussels.'

That figured. No Parisian would dream of living in a small Belgian town. They consider Brussels provincial enough.

I watched him drive off, smiling to myself. I might very well take a drive out to Ottignies one afternoon.

Hortense reappeared down the stairs a foot at a time, round-eyed with incredulity, tail nearly back to normal size.

'So there you are, Furry-Face,' I said severely. 'No Victoria Cross for you.'

And then I remembered the bad news. Uncle Edward was coming to stay.

Chapter 2

If I were writing a family history, I'd describe my uncle Edward as a gentleman-explorer. A century ago, he'd have been hacking his way through darkest Africa in a solar topee and a long beard, and delivering learned lectures to the Royal Geographical Society. He and my father never got on. My father is a born academic, a grave, measured man, while Edward is dynamic, witty, a dreadful flirt, and insatiably interested in just about everything.

I suppose Father felt a sense of responsibility, being seven years older. He'd been through the war, while Edward just missed it. Father had already made his way in academic circles, was laying down the foundations of a quiet, respectable, studious life and was prepared to make every effort to help his younger brother do the same, no matter how much of a rattle he thought him.

The only trouble was, Edward wasn't having any. The day he got his doctorate, he packed his bag, took the train to Marseilles and disappeared for eight months, during which time he went all round the Middle East on a camel. Father wasn't amused. He was even less amused when Edward vanished again the following year, this time into East Africa. When his money ran out, which was rather soon, Edward applied for research grants and went on travelling. 'Edward's latest expedition' was a constant feature of my childhood. He'd spend ten months of the year hiking through the Kalahari desert or canoeing down the Amazon, and turn up again bronzed, cheerful and broke at the family home just when we least expected him, with instant demands to be fed.

'Your uncle Edward is completely unreliable,' my mother would tell me with her measured French accent, a frown between her arched black brows. And Father would look even more serious and shut himself up in his study till the disturbing element had taken itself off again.

To be fair to Edward, he's actually a naturalist of some repute, being the discoverer of an undistinguished insect known as *Gryllulus haycastellani* or, for those without the benefit of a classical education, Haycastle's cricket. He has also written a few travel books, perhaps rather too erudite to appeal to the mass market. Edward is nothing if not an elitist.

I found myself smiling against my will, thinking about the amazing presents he used to send me when I was a kid: carved wooden gazelles from the Nairobi market, little boxes inlaid with mother-of-pearl from Aden, tiny sandalwood elephants which always lost their fragile tusks in transit and, on one occasion, a real weaver-bird's nest which I insisted on hanging up in my room and which disintegrated gradually all over the carpet for years. My mother sighed and said nothing. He once sent a box of coral-reef shells from Mombasa, which some idiot postman dropped on our front path, and the whole lot was smashed to bits the size of a sixpence.

'Just like Edward,' my mother said, looking darkly at the mess. 'Why can he not be sensible and send things that do not break?'

But Edward could no more be sensible than an enraged bull elephant can be considerate. I remember him descending on my respectable South of England girls' boarding school one weekend and sweeping me off, to the utter envy of my mates, to spend the day rooting round the dig of a Roman villa tucked away in the sunny chalk downs. That got me loads of Brownie points in the fifth form, I can tell you.

Then when I was eighteen and my mother sent me to stay with stuffy relatives in Paris for a month, and I was utterly miserable, it was Edward who miraculously appeared and, taking pity on me, broke his journey and showed me a glorious Paris totally different from the self-satisfied, snobbish world of the sixteenth *arrondissement*. He taught me about art, literature, history, food, wine and having fun, and even gave me a few useful tips about how to deal with snotty French cousins.

'Poke 'em in the nose, Matilda,' he said, 'poke 'em in the nose.'

I've been taking his advice ever since.

That really did it as far as my parents were concerned. There was a huge row of which I heard only the echoes, and Edward was sent packing, presumably for corrupting youth and taking my mind off my university career.

After that there were no more treats, but I was at university anyway, and later I left England to start hacking my own way through the jungle. I heard about Edward only through the odd comment in my mother's letters, or, now and then, in the newspapers. He was still dancing round the world with unflagging enthusiasm at the advanced age of sixty-five.

I hadn't seen him for more than fifteen years. I wasn't even sure I wanted to. What would he be like now? From the voice on the phone, he hadn't changed a bit. Still casual, still demanding, still perfectly sure of his welcome.

I spent the afternoon making grudging preparations, my irritation redoubling while I resentfully dusted, made up beds and bought food. I hate domesticity.

Fortunately the house is kept in good order by Yasmina, my weekly cleaning lady, so only a superficial tidy-up was required. Even so, time got away from me and I was late getting to the station, and then I couldn't find a place to park. I hate arriving anywhere hot and bothered.

The Gare du Midi was being renovated, and consequently was in total chaos, with dust, dirt and heaps of bricks everywhere. Half the concourse was partitioned off with orange and white tape. The big TV screens showing arrivals and departures were *en panne* and knots of passengers were crowding round the printed notices on the walls. There were hordes of people: a large group of wolf-cubs off to camp in the Ardennes, families coming back from the coast with buckets and spades, Club Med types with expensive, artificially induced tans and Louis Vuitton luggage, the inevitable rash of summer back-packers and, heaped in a corner, the cross-Channel contingent from the Ostend train.

There had been summer storms in the Channel, and the survivors were all recognizable by their colour: a delicate shade of pistachio. A couple of dozen unfledged bolshy fifteen-year-olds in scruffy approximations of school uniform were slumped on the dirty tiled floor, moaning dismally and ignoring their harassed teacher's exhortations to get up or they'd miss the coach. Next to them a distraught young mother was trying to control a struggling, wailing baby, while her small son was resignedly being sick – with considerable presence of mind under the circumstances – into his Mickey Mouse cap. Oh, the joys of cross-Channel travel.

I looked round for my uncle. He wasn't difficult to locate. It was the voice: clear, authoritative and with the kind of accent that used once to be described as 'BBC'.

'Of course she'll be here,' he was saying, bending

11

over a huddled figure on a bench. 'Matilda won't let us down. She's my niece, after all.' And then he turned round and saw me.

He hadn't changed much, I suppose. Tall, like all us Haycastles, and still thin as a hop-pole. He'd been startlingly good-looking as a young man. The thick golden hair had thinned and faded, and the long face was seamed and rather leathery under its tan; it was like looking at a photograph through a thin film of tissue-paper. But for all that it was the same face. And it was definitely the same smile which appeared instantly and startlingly, and the same white teeth, all still apparently his own.

'My beautiful niece,' he said.

Do you shake hands with an uncle you haven't seen for years? Do you embrace? I didn't know. Neither did he. We both hesitated, and then it was too late to do anything. I glanced down at the third party: a big young man, by the look of the powerful shoulders, doubled up and apparently incapacitated.

'Who's Superman?' I asked.

'My research assistant,' said Edward. 'He's under the weather. The Channel was rather choppy.'

'I thought only MPs had research assistants,' I said. 'Can he walk?'

'We'll give him a hand.' Edward bent to take a firm grip under one of the sufferer's arms. 'I keep telling him he'll feel much better when he's had a hot meal.'

That happens to be true, but it's the last thing you want to hear when you've just spent four hours talking to the great white telephone, courtesy of the cross-Channel ferries. I slipped my hand under the other arm and heaved, and we got Superman to his feet. He was husky and blond, and the green hue was beginning to fade slightly.

'Luggage?' I asked.

'I'll get it. Can you hang on to him?'

12

I found myself staggering under Superman's considerable weight while my uncle rounded up two large suitcases.

'If we take one each, and support Byron with the other hand, we'll only have to make one trip,' my uncle said briskly. 'Ready – LIFT!'

Byron? The sufferer raised his head and muttered: 'Real sorry, ma'am,' and all was made clear. An American.

'Matilda, I said LIFT,' came my uncle's plaintive voice.

I could either argue or lift. I lifted. Together we staggered out of the station and made our painful way towards the car. I hoped it would still be there. The Gare du Midi's in a dodgy area. I hoped we'd all fit in.

Back home, we lugged the research assistant up three flights of stairs and dumped him in the guest room. He wasn't taking much notice, but his round, ingenuous face was looking rather rosier.

'He'll be fine in a few hours,' my uncle said, bending to pull off the young man's large shoes. 'A glass of milk and a sandwich would do him good.'

'Probably,' I agreed, heading for the door. I wasn't proposing to play Florence Nightingale up and down the stairs all night.

Down in the kitchen, I opened the fridge to see about supper, and Hortense uncloaked at my feet, being able, like all cats, to detect a fridge door opening at a distance of several hundred light-years. My uncle appeared in the doorway.

'I brought you this,' he said, waving a bottle of Veuve Clicquot. 'It's a bit warm. Got an ice-bucket?'

'Are frogs waterproof? This is your niece, remember. Look in the sideboard. Is chicken OK for supper?'

'Ah.' He paused, the ice-bucket in his hands. 'I never thought to let you know. I'm a vegetarian these days.'

'Since when?' I stared at him, remembering the

many glorious gourmet meals of the past.

'Five years ago. If you're going to commit yourself to protecting animals, it seems a bit dastardly to go round eating them as well.'

He shoved the champagne into the ice-bucket and sat down at my kitchen table, leaving three ice-cube trays dead on the draining board. His logic was flawless, but now I had a freezer full of useless meat.

'Never mind,' said Edward comfortingly, 'I'm sure Byron will eat it all up. Appetite like a horse, that boy.'

'Who is he? What do you need a research assistant for anyway?'

'He turned up in London three months ago and positively begged me to take him on and I couldn't refuse. I used to know his mother.'

I couldn't resist it. 'One of the popsies?' I asked.

Edward's 'popsies', of whom there were legions, had been yet another cause of family disapproval. I'd started a catalogue once, but had given up at the age of fifteen.

Edward looked indignant. 'Certainly not. We were colleagues. Dr Jo-Ann Henderson. We were doing field research together. Thirty years or so ago. She was a professor at one of those American universities. Married a vet and the result was Byron T. Kaplan.'

I had to laugh. Byron T. Kaplan!

'He's writing a paper on the European colonization of Africa,' Edward went on. 'So I thought a trip to Belgium might be useful for him. He's been a real help with organization and all that. Trouble is, he's rather accident-prone, but I suppose he can't help it. His mother was just the same.' His eye fell on Hortense, who was still sitting hopefully by the fridge. 'Is that your puddy-canat?'

It was the first time for years that I'd heard that endearingly silly childhood term, and I had to smile.

'Her name's Hortense,' I said. 'Watch out, she's suspicious of strangers.'

14

He made a chirping noise and patted his knee invitingly, and Hortense immediately leapt on his lap and starting rubbing her head against his chest, purring like mad. He tickled her under the chin, murmuring idiotic blandishments into her black velvet ears.

'Don't be fooled by the Shirley Temple routine,' I said sourly. 'That cat is four kilos of cunning in a black fur coat.'

Edward grinned. Hortense turned round a couple of times and settled down happily, still singing away.

'How long are you staying?' I asked.

'It rather depends on you. I thought a few days – maybe a week. In fact, I've got an arrangement to suggest.'

I tested the champagne, which was cooling nicely. 'OK,' I said, sitting. 'What's it all about?'

'I'm attending an international conference on conservation – making a couple of presentations and chairing a Round Table. It starts Thursday and runs through to Sunday. I thought that if you're not busy, you might like to do some secretarial work for me – helping with the speeches and chauffeuring us about and so on. I'll pay the same rate you'd be getting from your agency. There'll be a few free drinks and dinners and things too. How about it?'

'Can you afford me?' I asked. 'Five hundred francs an hour. Special rate for uncles. You don't tell the tax people and neither do I.'

'Done,' he said. 'How's the champers?'

'Coming along. Where's the conference being held?'

'Some brand new meeting centre somewhere in town – I'll have to get the papers and look it up. Well, now that's settled, how about a drink? My tongue's been hanging out for twenty minutes.'

Half a bottle of champagne undoubtedly slows down one's reactions, so when my mother called later and asked in her cool way if Edward were there, I didn't

15

at first understand the grimaces and negative arm-wavings from the chair opposite.

'Yes, he's here,' I said, and held out the receiver, realizing at the same moment that he didn't want to speak to her. Too late.

He took the phone reluctantly and said in a tentative voice: 'Hello, Claire.'

I moved away to the window and looked out into the garden. Hortense was leaping wildly around after gnats in the gathering twilight, while a small grey-and-white cat crouched admiringly under the cotoneaster. This was Minette, the cat next door, Hortense's sidekick, and the only other feline allowed in the house and garden.

Behind me there was a tense semi-silence, punctuated by my uncle saying 'Yes', 'No' and 'Of course not' at intervals. He sounded supremely uncomfortable. Finally he said: 'Your mother would like a word,' and held the receiver out to me with a grimace of relief.

'Really, this is absolutely typical of Edward.' My mother sounded quite cross. 'Matilda, if it is not convenient for you to have him there, tell him so and ask him to leave. There are plenty of perfectly good hotels in Brussels and he is quite able to afford them. I do not understand why he is imposing himself on you. I have told him so.'

It was Edward's turn to move away to the window and stare out.

'There's no need to get agitated,' I said. 'I'm going to do a bit of work for him and he's going to pay me, so I'm sure it'll work out quite well.'

'But to appear out of the blue like this – it is the limit. And you know how Malcolm and I feel about him.'

It's characteristic of my mother that she never shortens anybody's name. We are Malcolm, Edward and Matilda to her and shall be till the end of time.

16

'I really don't mind,' I said patiently. 'It's no big deal. They won't be any trouble.'

'They?' said my mother, her voice throbbing over the line.

'He's brought his research assistant.'

'What research assistant?' my mother asked sharply. 'He has not dared to bring one of his . . .' She stopped, searching for the right word.

'No, no.' I tried not to laugh. 'It's a young man. An American. Honestly, there's no need to worry. They're only staying for a few days.'

'Well, it's up to you, I suppose. *Mais je te préviens – ils vont s'incruster.* And tell Edward to be careful.'

'Why?' I asked, surprised, but she'd already rung off. I turned to my uncle. 'She thinks you're going to stay for ever. And she said to be careful. What does she mean?'

'I haven't the foggiest,' said Edward. 'Not exactly overjoyed about it, is she? Well, Matilda, do you want me to leave?'

'You can't. We made a deal. I've drunk your champagne.'

'Your mother . . .'

'My mother's got her knickers in a twist over nothing,' I said. 'I know they don't approve of you, but I'm old enough to make up my own mind. You'll have to share the room with Superman, though. I hope he doesn't snore.'

'No, he doesn't,' Edward said, suddenly twinkling. 'But I do.'

It was going to be all right, I thought to myself after Edward had taken himself off to bed and I was clearing up. It might even turn out to be rather fun. I was wrong, as it happened, but champagne has a tendency to make me over-optimistic.

17

Chapter 3

The first thing I was aware of next morning was the smell of coffee and toast filtering up from downstairs. I thought I was dreaming at first, but on second sniff it was real enough. I got out of bed, pulled on a pair of trousers and a T-shirt and went to investigate.

The kitchen table was neatly laid for three, with cups, crockery, utensils and the paper napkins I keep for special occasions, such as Christmas. Margarine, marmalade and honey were grouped tidily in the middle of the table. The coffee machine was doing overtime in its corner, and as I entered the kitchen, the toast leapt out of my old toaster with a merry ping.

'Well . . .!' I said.

I knew it wouldn't be Edward. Domesticity isn't his strong point either. It was Byron T. Kaplan bending over the sink, yellow rubber-gloved hands in the soapy water, doing last night's washing-up. He turned, dripping all over the floor, and gave me a schoolboy's smile, half-shy, half-pleased.

'Morning, ma'am. Just thought I'd help out. I hope you don't mind.'

I love American country accents.

'Mind?' I said. 'Men who wash up without being asked are rarer than unicorns. Carry on. Is Edward around?'

'Still asleep.' Byron T. turned back to the sink. He looked to be in his late twenties, built like an American

18

football player with lots of muscle across the shoulders. The face was open, with trusting blue eyes and a healthy open-air bloom. Fair hair stuck up slightly like a schoolboy's.

The coffee machine was still gurgling fit to burst. Byron T. pulled the plug out of the sink.

'Your sink doesn't drain too well,' he said, watching the suds swirl round. 'Would you like me to take a look? I'm sure I can fix it. I'm real good at that sort of thing.'

'Be my guest,' I invited. 'You look a whole lot better than last night. Did you sleep well?'

He shot me a sideways look, rather cautiously.

'Well, Dr Haycastle is rather a restless sleeper.' He pulled off the rubber gloves, wiped his hands on a tea-towel, then picked up the coffee pot and poured me a cupful. Some of it spilt in the saucer.

'You mean he snores,' I said, taking the cup.

He gave me another cautious look, then suddenly grinned. 'Yes, I guess I do mean that.'

'Move the bed into the other spare room on the first floor. I've got my computer in there, but we can bring it downstairs for the time being.'

'Thank you, ma'am, I will.'

'You can forget the "ma'am",' I said. 'My name's Matilda.'

'That's fine with me.' He poured his own coffee and sat down, rocking the table. I half expected him to say grace. Instead he stared at me. I became aware that I hadn't combed my hair, and shifted uneasily.

'I'm sorry,' said Byron T., blushing slightly. 'It's just that you're so much like your uncle – has anyone ever told you that?'

'Frequently.' I reached for the toast. 'The family resemblance is proverbial. How long have you been with him?'

'A couple of months. I'd heard so much about

19

him and I just nagged and nagged at Mom till she agreed to write him a letter and then I came over and pestered him till he said he'd take me on.'

'I bet he's paying you peanuts,' I said, my mouth full of toast.

'It's not the money. It's the Experience. And when I heard he was coming to Belgium, well, I was just delighted. It's a chance to research the whole Congo thing at first hand.' He looked round happily. 'This is a really great house. Is it yours?'

'Rented,' I told him. 'It belongs to a friend of mine. He's in Afghanistan with Médecins Sans Frontières.' I saw the puzzled frown and translated.

'Oh,' said Byron T. Then he frowned again and added: 'Don't you have to go to the office today? Or are you on vacation?'

'No. I'm on the payroll now, same as you. Edward needs a secretary.'

Byron T. reached for the marmalade and somehow managed to knock the jar over. As it rolled away he made a wild grab to save it, rocking the table violently. Coffee spilled from our full cups. Byron T. leapt up with an anguished look on his face.

'It's OK,' I said, getting up too. 'Sit down. I'll clean up.'

'Sorry,' he said ruefully. 'I'm just clumsy, I guess. Mom's always telling me that.'

We settled down again, just as Hortense strolled into the kitchen with a loud demand for breakfast. Byron T. sneezed violently. Hortense and I looked at him in amazement as he sneezed again and again, struggling to pull a hanky out of his trouser pocket, which can be difficult if you're sitting down.

'Sorry,' he managed to gasp between sneezes. 'I'm allergic . . . to cats.'

I tried and failed to persuade Hortense to have her breakfast outside, and in the end it was Byron T. who

20

retreated into the garden with his coffee and toast. The din had wakened my uncle, who was positively bouncing with energy. He was unsympathetic about Byron T.'s affliction.

'He'll just have to keep his door closed,' he said. 'Or maybe we could get him desensitized. Or perhaps a surgical mask?'

He seized the marmalade and helped himself liberally.

'We'll start on my presentation after breakfast,' he said, taking a large bite of toast. 'I've got it all worked out in my mind so it shouldn't take long.'

The sound of the key in the front door and a cheerful voice saying: *'Bonjour Mathilde,'* heralded the arrival of my cleaning-lady, Yasmina, eighteen years old, black-eyed, sharp as a knife-blade and merry as a forestful of birds. When I introduced her to Edward I was amazed. He started off in competent though unashamedly British French, such as is used by Douglas Hurd and members of the Royal Family, but in five minutes he'd switched to rusty Arabic, and by Yasmina's smiles and laughter and exclamations, he was doing all right.

It took some time, but we did manage to get down to work eventually, with Yasmina's singing and the muted hum of the vacuum cleaner as accompaniment. Edward had a speech scheduled on the first morning, and another on Saturday afternoon. He paced up and down dictating, with suitable hand-gestures, while I typed straight onto the computer, and Byron T. sat surrounded by various reference books, ready to verify statements and provide quotations, and sneezing from time to time.

I soon realized that Edward's literary style tended towards the purple. He got peeved when I pointed this out.

'I could put it all in words of one syllable if you

absolutely insist,' he said, sharply. 'But this isn't a TV audience, you know.'

'That's not the point,' I countered. Byron T. looked from one to the other of us, biting his lip. 'The simpler you keep it, the more you get across. Look at David Attenborough.'

'Don't you mention that man to me,' said my uncle, in rising exasperation, throwing his notes down on the floor. 'All I ever hear is David Attenborough this and David Attenborough that. What's David Attenborough got that I haven't?'

'Good looks, intelligence, wit, charm and enthusiasm,' I said dryly. 'And you can understand every word he says.'

There was a moment's frosty silence, then, unexpectedly, Edward chuckled. 'Point taken.' He bent to pick up his notes. 'I admit it – I just like long words. Tell you what, Matilda, you can go through afterwards and polish it up. How about that?'

'OK.' I peered at the screen. 'You were about to tackle over-population.'

'Ah yes,' said Edward. 'They won't like this, but too bad. Somebody's got to tell 'em. One day there'll be nothing on this planet except people, cars and industrial effluent, and they'll all be wondering how it happened.'

The phone rang. I answered. A woman asked to speak to Dr Haycastle.

'The secretary of Philippe Andrieu,' I said, holding the receiver out, and then frowned. Where had I heard that name before? Edward backed away, making waving motions with his hands. What was it about him and telephones?

I put on my senior secretary voice and told the appropriate lie: 'Dr Haycastle is in a meeting right now. May I take a message?'

The voice had hard, accusatory, teutonic intonations.

'I have been trying to contact him for two weeks and I do not know why but I always seem to miss him. We need copies of his presentations. We have needed them for three weeks and the conference begins tomorrow. This is most urgent.'

Light dawned. 'Are you organizing the conference?' I asked.

'Monsieur Andrieu is the conference chairman,' she said. 'Would you please check with Dr Haycastle?'

I checked with Dr Haycastle, who frowned.

'Didn't send them,' he said. 'Haven't written them yet.'

I relayed the information over the phone, suitably abridged, and heard a despairing wail. 'But what are we going to do? I must make copies for all the delegates by tomorrow morning.'

'We're preparing the speeches now,' I said. 'I'll bring you the papers first thing tomorrow and you can make the copies during the day.'

There was a long, anguished silence.

'Very well,' she said finally. 'I suppose that will have to do. I will be there at eight-thirty tomorrow morning. Please ask for Madame Müller.'

I put the phone down 'Who's Philippe Andrieu?'

Edward looked up at me for a moment, then replied, turning away as he spoke: 'Conference organizer. Belgian businessman.'

I remembered then. 'He owns an animal shelter called Les Fauves?'

'That's the man.' Edward was searching for something among the papers on the floor.

'Do you know him?' I asked.

'Slightly. Do you mind if we get on with this or I'll lose my train of thought.'

I abandoned Philippe Andrieu and concentrated. Edward was on form, and we got the stuff finished and printed out by evening. We had supper. Edward went

23

out in the garden to play with the cats and Byron T. leapt into action with the washing-up.

'You don't have to do that,' I protested.

'I know. But I want to.'

'Your mother certainly trained you well. Thanks very much.'

'No problem. Mom would appreciate the compliment.' There was a short pause, then he glanced at me and said, frowning slightly: 'I don't want you to get the idea I'm criticizing, and please don't say anything to Dr Haycastle, but don't you think – maybe – his views on over-population are a mite extreme?'

'A mite,' I said.

'All that stuff about the Four Horsemen of the Apocalypse,' Byron T. pursued gloomily, 'and famine and disease being Nature's way of checking rampant growth and we oughtn't to interfere. And that bit about humanitarian aid being a waste of money – I mean, people aren't going to like that, are they?'

'Probably not.' I was used to my uncle's politically unacceptable views. What's more, I knew from experience that pleas to be reasonable would fall on deaf ears.

'Hadn't we better say something, then?' Byron T. said, turning from the sink.

'Why?' I asked. 'After all, he's entitled to his own point of view, no matter how eccentric. And it'll give them something to talk about.'

'I guess you're right.' Byron T. turned reluctantly back to the sink. 'It's just that – well, he had a few nasty letters from British people who didn't agree with him.' He paused for a moment, then added sepulchrally: 'Threats!'

'What sort of threats?' I asked, startled.

'Just telling him to watch out. He didn't take them seriously.' He paused again. Why did I get the feeling there was more?

24

'Then there was the accident,' said Byron T. in a voice of doom.

'What accident?' I enquired resignedly.

'He nearly got himself knocked down by an automobile. Just last week. He reckons it had nothing to do with the letters, but I'm not so sure. He gets awful mad if I mention it. He thinks I'm fussing about nothing.'

I didn't like the sound of this at all. Was this why my mother had told him to be careful? What else was he not telling me? I looked out into the garden, my irritation returning. Edward was lying full-length on the lawn with Hortense standing on his chest. I hoped his clothes were ant-proof.

Chapter 4

We were up bright and early next day for the conference. At least, Byron T. was bright and early. He made American pancakes with maple syrup for breakfast, and was as cheerful as a little sunbeam. Edward and I were rather less bright. Getting up early doesn't suit us. But the timetable said Registration and Coffee at 9 a.m., so at ten before the hour we were pulling into the brand-new car park of the brand-new Burgundia Conference Centre.

It was located in the wedge-shaped area of land between the Liège motorway and the Boulevard de la Woluwe. The fringes of Brussels are constantly moving outwards, with office blocks and hotels seeding like dandelions, undeterred by the recession. This was one of the busiest building areas, conveniently near the airport, with a number of major companies located along the big main road to Zaventem.

The conference centre was so new the shine wasn't off it yet. The landscaped garden round the building was raw with sand, full of recently planted little shrubs still struggling to take hold. The building itself consisted of a five-star hotel, a fitness centre with swimming pool, and the conference facilities. It was several storeys high and star-shaped, made of smoked glass with shiny bands that reflected the sky.

We walked into a marble atrium which held a forest of *ficus benjaminas* reaching up to a big clear-glass

26

ceiling. Huge reception desks stood to either side, with smiling female androids in cerise uniforms behind them. In the centre, a wide, shallow double stairway curved up to the rest of the complex, on either side of a marble pool with goldfish and a fountain.

'Jiminy crickets,' said Byron T., gaping.

I, however, had seen this kind of thing before. I looked round and spotted a sign with a hand on it pointing to the Salle Philippe le Hardi, where our conference was taking place. I steered my party that way.

As we reached the foot of the stairs, two people appeared at the top, talking. One was a tall woman in a yellow suit with a clipboard in her hands. The other was a dark man. On seeing us he advanced smilingly with his hand held out and said, in English with only a slight accent: 'Dr Haycastle. What a pleasure to see you again after all this time.'

He was tall, thin and beautifully dressed. In his sixties, I thought, looking at the pale-skinned, patrician face, but the only signs of age were a weariness round the eyes and a slightly receding hairline. He looked intelligent and authoritative.

I glanced enquiringly at my uncle. Edward's face was white, the mouth set, the eyes glittering. His hands were clenched at his sides. 'I don't shake hands with murderers,' he said, in a clear voice that carried to every part of the atrium. Then he pushed past the outstretched hand and pressed on up the stairs.

There was a ghastly silence. A dozen people were present. All had their mouths open, including me. The dark man lowered his hand, gave a half-apologetic smile, shrugged his elegant shoulders and resumed his descent, together with the lady in yellow. Full marks for style. But what on earth did Edward think he was up to?

I raced up the stairs in pursuit of my errant relative and found myself in another large reception area. This one didn't rate a fountain. There were two cerise-clad automatons behind another desk, and on the far side of the room a long table with a white cloth and all the doings for breakfast. Half a dozen delegates were standing about sheepishly, drinking coffee and hoping to see someone they knew. On one side, large double doors opened into what was obviously the conference room.

I was hailed by one of the Barbie dolls at the check-in desk, a pretty child with the charm button switched to FULL. I gave my name. As I received my badge and conference file, a staccato voice called out: 'Miss Haycastle? Is that you? I am Ilse Müller.'

I turned, surprised. I'd forgotten all about her. She was a tall bony woman in her early fifties, with spectacles hanging on chains and a silk scarf coming undone round her thin neck. We were about the same height, but she stooped slightly. She looked worried. She looked as if that were her habitual expression.

'Do you have the papers?' she asked. 'Dr Haycastle's papers?'

'Oh yes,' I said, remembering. I fumbled in my briefcase and handed over the goods. She put her specs on her nose and flicked anxiously through them.

'Thank you very much.' Her voice was abrupt. 'There is so much to do and the people here are so slack, they have not provided what we asked for. And the microphones do not work.'

'I expect they just need to be connected up.' I tried to edge away, my eyes scanning the horizon.

'But they should have been ready,' Ilse Müller insisted. 'I asked most especially that it should be so. I have to do everything myself. And there is nobody here – the conference manager has not arrived yet. It is really too bad.'

Behind us, a woman said: 'You were asking for me, Madame Müller?' and we both turned. The lady in the yellow suit stood there, her clipboard in the crook of

28

her arm, clasped to her immaculate jacket front. Smooth dark hair framed an oval face with wide-spaced blue eyes and a well-defined mouth. She was about my age – mid-thirties. She looked confidently in charge.

'I understand you have some problems?' she said.

Ilse Müller was obviously one of those people who go through life convinced that the entire world is conspiring against them.

'I really must say that I expected better service than this, Madame Ryckmans,' she began complainingly. 'Nothing works and there are no technicians here. I specifically left instructions that everything should be ready and now the microphones are not connected. And there are not enough bottles of water on the speakers' table, and I'm sure I asked for the pale blue tablecloth, not the dark blue.'

The woman in yellow didn't bother to be tactful. She consulted her notes briefly and said: 'Facilities for eight speakers were requested by telefax, and the dark blue tablecloth. Here's your signature at the bottom of the page.' And she held out the clipboard, a small, triumphant smile on her lips.

For casual nastiness, it was hard to beat. Ilse Müller flushed an unhealthy dry red. The woman in yellow said lightly: 'The technicians will be here in a moment. Will that be all?' She paused, then went on: 'Please let me know if there's anything else.' We watched her move away, her walk smooth and unhurried. She reminded me of a leopardess, but maybe I was insulting the leopard family.

'Who's that?' I asked.

'Monique Ryckmans,' Ilse replied, her voice trembling. 'The conference manager. She is always like this. I have been bending over backwards to make sure they have had all the right instructions and then this happens. It is really heartbreaking.'

I wondered if a hint on how to make tactful complaints would be appreciated, and decided it probably wouldn't. Anyway, I hadn't the time.

'Don't let her upset you,' I said, starting to move away. I had problems of my own. Where *was* Edward?

I tried the *salle de conférence*. It was a big, big room; I guessed it could hold up to eight hundred people. At the back there were interpreters' cubby-holes and a projection booth. The walls were panelled in imitation oak, and the comfortable-looking chairs were turquoise blue, a shade darker than the carpet. The auditorium sloped down to a dais, upon which there was a long table with a dark blue cloth, glasses and bottles of mineral water set out. On either side was a speaker's rostrum with microphone. Behind was a large screen. Edward wasn't there.

Outside, there was now a crowd round the breakfast table. A couple of glittering saris here, a cluster of brilliant African prints there formed dashes of bright colour among the sober business suits of the Europeans. No sign of the amazing disappearing uncle.

Should I check out the gentlemen's loo? I was about to dash back to the hotel foyer when a general drift began into the conference room. I abandoned the idea. I waited till all the delegates were in, then made an unobtrusive entrance and sat near the back. Long experience of meetings has taught me how useful it is to be able to slip out unnoticed. I caught sight of Byron T.'s fair head and solid shoulders a few rows forward. Eight people, including Philippe Andrieu, took their places on the dais. Then, at last, Edward came in and took a seat near the door. He didn't see me. He looked very stern.

The conference got under way. Welcome speech, acknowledgements, introductions, thanks. Requests for no smoking and no bleeping watches. The first speaker got up, clearing his throat, pushing his spectacles up, riffling through his papers. I groaned inwardly, recognizing the signs. The presentation was in German, read directly from a script and the speaker had a very monotonous voice. It lasted every one of thirty-five minutes. By the time he'd done, the Sandman and I were about to go away together. There was a burst of desultory clapping, and Philippe Andrieu rose and moved to the left-hand rostrum. I dragged myself up, stifling a yawn, and looked round. Edward had gone.

Expletive deleted. Forget the unobtrusive exit. I leapt up and shot out of the door, startling the delegates around me. Nobody in the foyer except one of the cerise dollies, sitting behind the desk filing her nails. She looked up and smiled as I dashed down the corridor, just in time to see Edward's trouser-leg disappear into the lift. The doors slid shut as I reached the button. A little light winked on the panel. He'd gone down to the basement.

I kept my finger on the button, but nothing happened. The lift didn't want to come up again. Muttering curses, I looked round wildly for the emergency staircase. It was down another, much less plush corridor and round a corner. The carpet petered out entirely at the foot of a bare grey door. I yanked it open and clattered down.

I emerged into a small underground car park, presumably for the use of the higher-ranking staff and very important guests. The lift doors were opening and shutting helplessly, blocked by a large green plastic dustbin. I saw Edward right across on the other side. He was standing beside a black Mercedes, a look of intense concentration on his face.

I couldn't believe what happened next. As I watched, he lifted his hand, which contained a heavy spanner, and brought it down sharply. There was a dull smashing sound, and all the lights on the car began to flash madly on and off, as if in protest.

What in Heaven's name was he playing at? Galvanized

by a sudden terrible vision of disgrace and retribution if he got caught, I threw myself across the car park and seized his arm. He had the car door open and was busy rooting about in the back seat. He turned an astonished face towards me.

'Get out of here at once!' he snapped, and continued rooting.

'Come on,' I yelled, tugging desperately. 'You'll get caught. For the love of Mike, come on.'

He straightened up, a thin black leather briefcase in his hand. He was wearing my rubber gloves. I suppose I should have been grateful he'd had the sense.

'I haven't finished,' he protested. He sounded perfectly sane. Maybe I was the one with the blown fuse.

'Out!' I snapped. 'Up the ramp. No arguments.'

He didn't want to go. I hauled him bodily away from the car towards the vehicle exit, still protesting. Luckily the outside doors weren't closed. There was just a red-and-white barrier and daylight beyond. We pounded out into the shadow of the building.

'Slow down,' my uncle said urgently, holding me back. 'We don't want to look suspicious. We'll just walk quietly across to your car.' Tucking the stolen briefcase under one arm, he took my elbow and strolled off with me across the car park. I was feeling as conspicuous as a magpie on a fence, but Edward might have been walking up the Champs Elysées. He took my car keys out of his pocket – at which my eyes popped more than somewhat – unlocked my car and said: 'Get in and drive.'

'Where? I asked stupidly.

'Anywhere.'

I drove.

Beside me, Edward emptied the briefcase of the papers it contained and scanned them swiftly. I glanced sideways. Embossed on the front of the briefcase were the initials PMA.

I twigged.

'What does the 'M' stand for?' I asked grimly.

My uncle didn't answer, but his mouth assumed a position that might have been a smile.

'Maurice,' he said. 'Stop here.'

I swerved to a stop near a deserted building-site. Edward got out and I watched him dump the briefcase behind a pile of bricks. Then he got in again. 'All right,' he said. 'Now back to the hotel. Oh, by the way, here's your spanner.'

My spanner?

'If you think you're going to get off without an explanation,' I said deliberately, 'you're greener than you're cabbage-looking.'

Our eyes locked.

'Not now.' he said. 'Later. I'm giving a presentation in thirty minutes. It'll look suspicious if we're not there.'

I considered. I saw his point. But all the same . . .

'You broke into Andrieu's car and stole from it.' I still could not quite believe it. 'And I've made myself an accessory. The story'd better be good. I'm not doing time for nothing.'

He smiled, rather faintly. 'You shouldn't have interfered.'

'People are always telling me that,' I snapped. 'Suppose there's a security camera in the garage? Suppose somebody saw us?'

'No cameras, I checked. Please, Matilda, I promise to tell you, but not now. Not now.'

There was a silence, during which I grimly struggled against my better judgement. 'OK,' I said. 'I'll take you back. But the explanation's only postponed.'

'That's my girl.'

When I glanced at him again, his eyes were closed and I thought from his expression that he was exhausted. However, by the time we got to the hotel his energy seemed to have come back. Inside all was peaceful. The break-in hadn't been discovered yet; nobody'd been down to the basement. I hoped I wasn't looking guilty.

My uncle gave his presentation with perfect and enviable calm and handled the lively question session with practised skill. I took ten minutes to reassure myself that the hotel really didn't have security cameras installed in the basement, or anywhere else for that matter. Edward then ruined lunch for me by saying: 'Don't eat too much. There's a dinner this evening. All the speakers are going.'

I stifled a wail. A formal dinner was the last thing I needed after the traumas of the day. And if Edward thought it was going to get him out of his explanation, he just didn't know how dogged I can be.

Chapter 5

'Right,' I said. 'You've got twenty minutes. Talk.'

I'd marched him grim-faced to the bottom of the garden and was standing facing him, arms folded. At the window above the kitchen, Byron T. could be glimpsed peering anxiously down at us.

Edward sighed and sat down on the garden steps.

'I don't know where to start.'

'Begin at the beginning,' I said, 'go on till you get to the end, and then stop.'

My uncle was silent for a moment. Then he said: 'I first came across him in Kinshasa in 1956. Leopoldville, it was then.'

'Andrieu?'

'The same. Do you know anything about the Congo?'

'A little.' I'd been out to the Royal Museum for Central Africa, a pleasant building set in the middle of a beautiful French formal garden in Tervueren village, and had wandered through the high dim halls looking at stuffed bongos and faded pictures of Victorian explorers. I said, reciting a lesson: 'The Congo Free State was founded in 1885 by King Leopold II as his own personal African playground. It became an official Belgian colony in 1908 when the king got into trouble over his treatment of the natives. Was systematically exploited in best colonial fashion till independence in 1960, whereupon a rather nasty rebellion broke out.

Now known as Zaire and doing no worse than most African countries and better than some.'

'That's about it,' said Edward. 'I went out there when the nationalist movement was just starting to take off. Anyway, that's neither here nor there. You know the Congo's enormously wealthy in terms of minerals – diamonds, copper, cobalt, radium, even uranium. Did you know there was Congolese uranium involved in the Hiroshima bomb?'

I didn't know.

'Anyway,' Edward went on, 'there was a lot of money to be made, colonists went out by the thousands, all kinds of companies sprang up. Not just in mining either – railways, banks, forestry, hydroelectric power, vegetable oil – even Unilever got in on the act. But Andrieu's family were in the mining business.'

He paused for a moment. 'He was a blackguard, even then. Led the high life: fast cars, women, all the colonial vices – and there were plenty, let me tell you. We crossed swords over one particular popsy and after that he went out of his way to make my life difficult.'

'What were you doing there?' I asked, curious.

'Trying to raise sponsorship for a trip to study pygmies. Andrieu really put a spoke in my wheel on that one. The colonists all stuck together, of course. Then I started hearing rumours about him – people were whispering about illegal trading in industrial diamonds and uranium. But there was something even more sinister. The mines were hugely labour-intensive and some of the recruiting methods used weren't exactly cricket. Andrieu had gangs going round kidnapping people and forcing them to work underground. There wasn't any proof, of course, but the natives certainly believed it. They hated him.'

'So what happened?' I asked. Hortense strolled through the hedge and leapt on to my knees with a flourish of her tail.

'Nothing, then. I managed to get my money elsewhere and off I went to do my study. I didn't think I'd run into him again.'

'But you did.'

'I did,' he agreed grimly. 'In '59 I was in Kenya, working on a wildlife project in the national parks. Big game poaching had been on the increase for several years and people were really starting to get worried. It was big business: all kinds of gangs and networks in operation and only a few game wardens in charge of vast acres of land.' He gave a bitter laugh. 'We were worried then, but my God, if we'd only known how bad things were going to get, I don't think we'd have had the heart to carry on.'

I said nothing, stroking Hortense's silken black fur. She purred happily, clasping my knees with steel grappling-hooks.

'They were after ivory, rhino horn, skins, tails – anything you can make souvenirs out of. They were killing thousands of wildebeest just to get their tails. Can you imagine the senseless stupidity of it? But the really big business was the ivory, of course.

'I was in Tsavo staying with Chris Parker, a friend of mine from university. He had a study project going on down there. He was crackers about animals – had a bungalow absolutely overrun with monkeys and gazelles and birds and various strays he'd picked up. A regular Saint Francis. The poaching upset him terribly – it upset us all. Anyway, the game wardens had organized an anti-poaching brigade and they were doing a gallant job, but we soon realized that there was one particular ring at work. The local tribesmen used to go out with poisoned arrows, but these chaps had jeeps and high-powered rifles. We found out a lot about them. The stuff wasn't going out through the usual route to Mombasa – it was going west to the Congo. And finally we got a few names.'

37

'Andrieu?' I asked.

Edward nodded. 'The very man. He was based in Nairobi then. Chris and I went up to make some investigations and we locked horns with him again. Not about a popsy this time. But it was the usual trouble – no proof. All we had was the word of a few frightened Africans and there was no way they'd ever testify in court. Then one day we heard that the poachers were out in our territory again. The wardens mounted an expedition and I decided to go with them. Chris stayed behind. We arrested a couple of men and rounded up a few kilos of ivory and then headed home.'

He stopped abruptly. I glanced at him and saw his face working as if what he was about to say was something he could hardly bear to contemplate, even after thirty-five years.

'They'd attacked Chris's bungalow while we were away. The house had been burned and all the animals slaughtered. And Chris had been hacked nearly to death with pangas.'

My hold on Hortense tightened, and she, not appreciating my sudden access of emotion, opened one awful golden eye and glared at me, dragon-like.

'He died that evening,' my uncle said abruptly. 'There was nothing we could do – he'd lost too much blood. We couldn't get him to hospital. But he was able to tell me that Andrieu was with the attackers and had stood and watched while the Africans did the dirty work.'

'What did you do?'

'There wasn't much we could do. No one else was there when Chris told me and there was no proof, never any goddamned proof. Our hands were tied. We did manage to throw some of the lower elements of the ring in the clink, but we couldn't touch Andrieu.'

'And that's why you're here now?'

He nodded.

'I've been following Andrieu's career on and off for

years. I'm a hundred per cent certain he's still involved in the animal trade. What's more, his circle of activity has become world-wide. Communications are so much easier now, and since the animals are getting scarcer, the prices are going up. Tiger bones, rhino horn, ivory, live rare animals – anything that pays, he sells. So when I saw he was organizing this conference, I thought this might be a last chance to get proof and nail the bastard once and for all.'

'Why didn't you tell me?'

'I didn't want you to get into trouble.'

'So you thought you'd just nip off and burgle Andrieu's car all on your own? By the way, did you find anything useful?'

He shook his head.

'Can I see?' I asked.

I waited while he fetched a sheaf of papers from the house. There wasn't much there. A copy of Andrieu's opening address, a printed brochure advertising the Burgundia Conference Centre, a gas bill, a list of delegates, a paperback book.

'What's this?' I asked, frowning, holding up the book.

It was *Vol de Nuit* by Antoine de Saint-Exupéry, in the Folio edition.

'Probably to stop him getting bored during the conference,' Edward said wryly. 'It's good stuff. Have you read it?'

'Years ago. Something about night pilots in South America, isn't it?'

As I opened the book, a folded piece of paper fluttered out. I caught it. A list of names: impala, oryx, okapi, gerenuk, bongo.

'Antelopes,' Edward said.

'Any significance?

'Not that I can see.' He sighed. 'The whole thing was a total waste of time.'

'Predictable enough. He'd be mad to keep anything

in his car. We're far more likely to find something at his home.' Then I remembered: 'Les Fauves! The animal shelter. That might be worth investigating. I've got an invitation. I met the director on Tuesday and he said I could visit any time.'

'What director?' Edward asked, frowning.

'Jean-Loup Perrault. He's from Paris. Just been appointed.' And he's gorgeous, I thought to myself, but I wasn't going to tell Edward that.

'So,' Edward said, 'you're not going to denounce me to the authorities after all?'

Not for the first time, I reflected that I must really be one sandwich short of a picnic. But what could I do? It seemed to run in the family.

'I'm going to help you investigate,' I said. 'Just promise not to break into any more cars. Incidentally, does all this have anything to do with the hate-mail and the accident in England?'

There was a brief, irritable silence. Then:

'Damn. Byron ratted,' Edward said testily. 'Of course it's got nothing to do with it. Cranks are always sending me anonymous letters, and the accident was just that – an accident. I wasn't looking where I was going.'

'Then why did my mother tell you to be careful?' I persisted.

'Because she thinks I'm five years old and need my nappies changed.'

'Did you still need your nappies changed at *five*?' I asked, innocently.

'I was a late developer.' Edward looked up at the window, where Byron T.'s anxious face was still to be seen.

'Let's keep this between ourselves for the moment,' my uncle said. 'It's not fair to lumber Byron with it. Also, his wits are apt to go woolgathering and he might give us away by mistake. I don't want to spend my declining years picking oakum.'

Chapter 6

I can't say that picking oakum would be my favourite retirement activity either. But injustice gets up my nose as much as it does the next person's. What's more, I reflected as I dressed at speed for dinner, if past experience was anything to go by, nothing short of an H-bomb would stop Edward on one of his crusades, so the best thing I could do was go along and limit the damage. Like preventing any more cack-handed attempts at burglary. Who did he think he was, Zorro?

My uncle stared at me as I came down the stairs and said: 'Isn't that frock a little skimpy? You'll catch cold in your chest.'

I ignored him, and also ignored Byron T., whose eyes were out on stalks. I suppose women don't have chests in America. Anyway, it was high summer.

We foiled Hortense's determined attempt to come with us, and piled once more into my car. I have to say that the springs were standing up to the strain manfully.

The restaurant was in an old monastery set in walled grounds with a stream running through them. Inside, it was all stone walls with stags' heads on them, and draughts. Luckily it was a warm evening. All the speakers and officials from the conference were present, many with spouses and assorted hangers-on. The tables were set for ten or twelve, with bright pink napiery and little glass bowls full of artificial flowers.

The first thing I did was bag a table at the edge of the room, which gave an excellent view of the proceedings. Among the tables was a pocket-handkerchief-sized dance floor, and a small bandstand with half a dozen musicians listlessly tuning up. Gradually people got themselves settled. Philippe Andrieu came in, elegant in black tie, with Monique Ryckmans at his side in a shimmering silk dress which had Christian Dior written all over it. I had to admit she was a beautiful woman. As I watched, she put her hand on his arm and said something with a smile which told me louder than shouting that their relationship was rather more than professional. Interesting.

A voice said in French: 'May we sit here?' and I turned in considerable surprise to see Jean-Loup Perrault smiling diffidently down at me. But of course, he worked for Andrieu, didn't he? I smiled, warm with pleasure, then suddenly caught sight of a young woman hovering behind him. Panic. Could he be married after all? But no. As they settled down, in the usual flurry of introductions, I gathered that she was Anny Baeke, his assistant at Les Fauves. She was short and rather plump, dressed in a long flowing robe of faded Indian cotton, with thong sandals. Her round, high-complexioned face was without make-up. She had curly hair the colour of brown sugar, and the large blue expressionless eyes of a porcelain doll. As she shook my hand, I caught a very faint, regrettable whiff of perspiration.

Most men look attractive in the formal black and white of a dinner-jacket. Jean-Loup looked sensational. He sat down beside me and said, smiling: 'I didn't make the connection between you and Dr Haycastle till I saw your names on the invitation list.'

'Well, I didn't know you were connected with the conference either. How's Elizabeth?'

'Getting on fine. Why don't you come and see her? Why don't you all come?' he added, looking up at

Edward and Byron T. My uncle was watching us with a slightly quizzical expression which I found irritating. Jean-Loup went on: 'The conference is only on in the morning tomorrow, and we're having an open day at the shelter in the afternoon. I'd be happy to show you round.'

'We'd be delighted,' my uncle said briskly. 'Wouldn't we, Matilda?'

We would indeed. As I thanked Jean-Loup, I noticed a rather sullen look on the face of Anny Baeke, who was sitting on his other side. Then my attention was distracted by the sight of Ilse Müller, who had arrived late, and was standing helplessly inside the door looking round for somewhere to sit. She was unbecomingly dressed in dull purple, with frills. This was an opportunity. I got quickly to my feet and hurried over.

'Madame Müller, don't you have a place? Why don't you come and join us?'

Burbling something about the fine weather, I led her back to the table and sat her down between my uncle and Byron T., introducing her as Monsieur Andrieu's personal secretary. I didn't have to say anything else. Edward caught on immediately. The charm switched on like searchlights, and in five minutes she was totally under the spell. I could hear her carping on about all the problems she'd been having, and Edward's soothing and sympathetic replies. I had to admit it; his technique hadn't suffered at all over the years.

'And on top of everything,' Ilse Müller wound up, 'Mr Andrieu's car was broken into. In the underground car park of all places. You would think at least it would be safe there. The security in that place is disgracefully lax!'

'Broken into?' my uncle said quickly.

We were all staring at Ilse. I hoped my face was registering the same surprise and shock as everyone else's.

'What was taken?' Byron T. asked, leaning forward.

'It is really terrible – Mr Andrieu is so concerned. There was a briefcase with some papers, but the bad thing is that there was a gun in the car and that was taken also. Of course we have had to call in the police. It is most disturbing.'

The shock and surprise on my face was absolutely genuine this time. I didn't dare look at Edward. As the *pâté maison* came round, I reflected that one thing was for sure – if we were found out, we were in even bigger lumber than I'd thought.

'That's odd.' Jean-Loup was frowning. 'There was a break-in at Les Fauves a month or so ago, before I arrived. Is this a problem in Brussels?'

'No more than in most big cities,' I told him. Which is true. At least you don't have to take your car radio inside with you in case it gets nicked, like you do in Paris. I went on: 'Who did it?'

'Vandals, apparently. It's difficult to see their motive. They broke into the office and smashed everything up. Set fire to the office records and destroyed the computer.'

'You've never seen such a mess,' Anny Baeke put in, leaning forward and craning round. 'Everything gone – all the files and invoices – everything.'

'You'll be having trouble with the tax-man next time round,' I said. 'Were the police any help?'

'They recommended we get a new security system,' Jean-Loup replied, rather ironically.

'Ah,' I said, 'the stable-door and horse approach. Typical. No fingerprints or clues?'

'Nothing,' Anny told me eagerly. 'They broke in at the back. The odd thing is, the alarm didn't go off. There's nobody around at night, of course.'

I found myself wondering about coincidences as we tackled our *poulet à l'estragon*.

The meal was lengthy, and as good as meals for large numbers of people ever can be. The band played

44

without much hope of being listened to, and the level of conversation steadily became deafening. The other half of our table had filled up with a delegation of Malaysians, who nodded and smiled politely at us and then chatted amongst themselves for the rest of the evening.

I decided it was my duty to draw out Jean-Loup and he didn't seem to mind, but I have to say, regretfully, that he was the most unflirtatious man I'd ever met. Indeed, he was unique, because Parisians are generally Olympic gold medal chatters-up. Don't get me wrong: he talked perfectly happily about animals, his work, travel and so on, totally ignoring Anny Baeke in order to concentrate on me. But that was it. No flirtatious looks or remarks, no small casual touches of the hand which are so easy when you're sitting together and the wine's been round a few times. It was, frankly, frustrating.

As dessert appeared Philippe Andrieu made a speech, which was short and, at our table, inaudible. The band broke into dance music, and a few brave souls got up to make exhibitions of themselves. As I put my dessert spoon down, I saw Andrieu and Monique Ryckmans dancing. They were clasped very close.

Two places away, Ilse Müller said venomously: 'That woman! Look at the way she behaves! That is what you must do to get the best jobs!'

Everyone turned towards her, startled. Leaning sideways, her face flushed and hair slightly disordered, she looked as if she'd put away too much second-rate claret.

Edward leaned over her with an interested air: 'The best jobs?' he enquired gently.

'Manager at the Burgundia. Her salary is twice mine, and I have been working for him for fifteen years. Fifteen years! And after everything I have done for him!'

45

Embarrassment deepened round the table. Everybody looked down at the tablecloth, except Edward, who rose to his feet and bent to offer Ilse his arm. 'Let's take a walk in the beautiful garden, my dear,' he suggested. 'Some fresh air will do us good. No, I insist. Come along.'

You'd have needed a will of iron to resist him, and Ilse Müller went quietly. She needed his arm to walk straight.

Jean-Loup said unexpectedly: 'Will you dance, Matilda?'

What do you think? We squeezed into the crowd on the minuscule dance floor and rocked sedately to and fro, which was as much movement as we could manage. He held me very correctly and said almost nothing. Over his shoulder, I could see Byron T. and Anny Baeke sitting at our table, separated by three empty chairs, both staring mutely at us. Why didn't they talk to one another? I thought, irritated.

The poor old band was just about getting into its stride when the party started to break up. Jean-Loup and I were soon left alone on the dance floor. We disengaged ourselves and returned rather slowly to our table, he clasping my hand loosely in his. Edward reappeared, alone. He'd poured Ilse Müller into a taxi and sent her home. It was time to go. We said our farewells, promising to see Jean-Loup the following day at the shelter.

Edward and I didn't say anything in the car, conscious of Byron T. half asleep in the back seat, but once we'd sent him upstairs to bed we repaired to the kitchen for a cup of tea and a discussion.

'What's all this about a *gun*?' I asked, putting the kettle on. 'Did you see a gun in the car?'

'To tell the truth, I didn't get much of a look. But I can't see Andrieu being stupid enough to leave one lying about.' He stopped abruptly, his eyes piercingly

46

blue. 'Unless he's caught on to what I'm doing and he's trying to implicate me in something serious. By God, that would be just like him, the ruffian!'

I must have looked incredulous, for Edward gave a short laugh and said: 'Oh yes, my dear. You don't know how devious he can be.'

'Ilse said that the police are in on it now,' I reminded him. 'What happens if they ask questions tomorrow? Are you going to own up?'

He looked at me. 'This may be my last chance to get Andrieu,' he said. 'I know it's asking a lot, but can you see your way to keeping it quiet? At least for the time being. I promise to set the record straight once I've got what I need.'

The trouble with family is that they're always asking you to go against your principles. But if the stories about Andrieu were true, then he deserved all he got. And I could hardly turn in my own uncle, could I. Could I?

'All right,' I said. 'But we'd better tell the same story if the police ask any questions. We went for a drive to get some fresh air and to polish up your speech. And please God nobody saw us coming out of the basement. What did you find out from Ilse?'

'Andrieu owns the Burgundia, the whole kit and caboodle, and he put Monique Ryckmans in charge of the conference centre. She's been his mistress for a year or two. Ilse's wildly jealous, of course. She kept hinting about nefarious goings-on, but she clammed up when I tried to get details. It might have been just the drink talking, and the jealousy.'

'She's his personal secretary. If anyone knows where the bodies are buried, she does. We ought to follow it up.'

'I'll find an opportunity tomorrow. It shouldn't be too difficult. How did you get on with your Wolfman?'

I smiled involuntarily at the soubriquet. 'Slowly.

Nothing suspicious so far. But I found out where he worked in Paris, so I can check up on him.'

'Well, we'll see tomorrow,' Edward said. 'God, I'm tired.'

That was an understatement of considerable magnitude. Thursday had lasted at least a week.

Chapter 7

Day Two. We had a thoroughly glum morning learning just how efficiently the human race is sawing off its own branch. None of the presentations was particularly histrionic; they didn't need to be. The hole in the ozone layer, the depletion of the oceans, the destruction of the rain-forest, the horrifying number of living species now under threat – all with one single cause: man. It was the soberest but most damning indictment of human stupidity I'd ever heard. As statistic after depressing statistic passed before my eyes, the eccentric crusade to which my uncle had dedicated his life seemed more and more heroic. The White Knight had metamorphosed into Parsifal.

Parsifal immediately destroyed his new image by doing the stupidest thing possible under the circumstances. The speeches had mercifully ended. I was gathering up my bits and pieces and thinking about lunch, when I heard raised voices. No, let's be accurate. Yelling. My uncle's voice. The conference room was emptying fast as people headed towards their food, but some of them were stopping and turning. I saw Byron T. looking round anxiously for me. I dashed down the aisle in time to see Andrieu break away and make for the exit, his face black with anger, followed by a distraught Ilse Müller. Edward, in contrast, was puce. Byron T. had him by the arm.

'That impertinent upstart!' My uncle was stuttering

with rage. 'How dare he presume to tell me what I can and can't say? It's censorship, pure and simple. Well, I put him in his place, the arrogant scoundrel!'

I had the other arm now. 'What happened?' I asked.

'He had the cheek, the Godalmighty cheek, to tell me that my presentation tomorrow might offend some of the more sensitive countries and that I had to cut out some of my remarks. Sensitive countries, my Aunt Fanny. He means it'll offend some of his cronies in the smuggling trade.'

He hadn't lowered his voice. I resisted the temptation to clap my hand over his mouth and hissed: 'For God's sake, shut up. Everybody's listening. Come on, let's get out of here.'

As I turned to hustle him down the aisle, a man rose from one of the nearby seats and said: 'Dr Haycastle?'

The tone was curt and the voice guttural, with a heavy accent. He was tall and bone-thin, with lank hair and a great wedge of a nose sticking out of a raw face which looked as if it had had a bad shave. He wasn't old. He wasn't smiling. He was wearing a grey raincoat. A raincoat? Inside? My stomach turned over.

'Inspector Guillaume,' he said. 'Brussels police.'

We stood frozen to the spot, like the Three Graces, though I don't suppose anyone would have paid seven million for us. My uncle's face had changed from puce to white. Byron T. was gaping. I was feeling green.

Inspector Guillaume produced an expression which looked remarkably like a sneer. 'An interesting little incident,' he said. 'You do not admire Monsieur Andrieu?' He was speaking to my uncle, but Matilda the Mouth got in first.

'It's not compulsory,' I said. 'What can we do for you?'

He didn't look at me directly. Instead I got a flickering sideways glance, furtive and hostile at the same time.

50

'I wish to ask some questions,' he said to my uncle. 'About the incident in the car park.'

'Oh,' replied Edward, rallying. 'Yes, of course. Whatever we can do to help.'

To my relief, the questions were routine. Where were you when the robbery took place, did you see anything suspicious, and so on. Byron T. had been in the conference room the whole time. Edward and I told our story. I hate lying – cocks were crowing at the tops of their voices all round. But Guillaume didn't seem suspicious. He thanked us grudgingly and left, giving me another of those glances. I had the feeling he thought he'd seen me before.

By common consent, we left the Burgundia and found somewhere else to have lunch. Nobody said much, Edward and I because of guilty consciences, and Byron T. because he was stuffing his face with the hugest pizza the restaurant could provide. He was having a bad day. He spilt tomato sauce and Parmesan on the floor and then trod in them. He knocked his glass of water into his *zuppa inglese*. Then as he got up to leave, there was a shrill yelp from under the table and a small pink poodle emerged shrieking in pain, to be immediately swept up to its indignant owner's bosom. If looks could kill, Byron T. would have been *ossobuco*. We got him out of there before he broke the place up and headed towards Ottignies.

It was a pretty ride through the Forêt de Soignes and past the lovely Lac de Genval which has the incongruous air of a seaside resort with its folly-like villas, boats and lakeside gardens. The animal shelter stood in its own grounds, a low white modern building with a landscaped approach, a large car park, and stables and enclosures at the back. There were already a number of cars parked; the open day was well under way. A family of four was just leaving, father carefully carrying a large cardboard box from which plaintive mews were issuing, children leaping about excitedly, mother looking apprehensive.

I studied the entrance critically as we went in. Double glass doors with a very new, businesslike lock on them. A very new, businesslike alarm system. A small glass cage just inside the doors, in which sat a nondescript white-haired man in an overall, who smiled and nodded at us as we went in. The stable door was well and truly shut.

Perhaps by chance, Jean-Loup came hurrying out almost immediately to greet us. He took my hand with reassuring eagerness. I was pleased to see him, too. Out of the corner of my eye, I saw that damned quizzical expression on Edward's face again. I decided to ignore it.

By previous family arrangement, I was speedily left alone with my Wolfman. We set off on a leisurely guided tour of the premises, with private commentary.

'An open day like this is a good opportunity for us to get some of these animals adopted,' Jean-Loup explained. We were talking French. I'd discovered the previous night that his English was minimal; the French aren't great linguists, one of the few characteristics they share with the English. 'We do specialize in exotic animals, as I told you before, but we also take in stray cats and dogs and injured wildlife. We have six salaried people working here, plus a number of volunteers who come in to help feed the animals and do basic maintenance tasks – cleaning the cages and so on.'

'You've managed to fix the damage done by the vandals?' I asked, looking round. Everything appeared quite normal.

'Yes, the office has been re-equipped, but all the computer data was lost and unfortunately we can't do anything about that.'

'Didn't anybody keep back-ups?' I enquired. The secretary talking. He looked puzzled – I think it was genuine.

'Valuable computer data should be backed up on to diskettes,' I explained. 'Then if your system crashes, or you get a virus, or an accident like this happens, at least your historical data's safe.'

Computer viruses were obviously a new form of wildlife to Jean-Loup. He shook his head and laughed ruefully.

'I'm afraid I don't know much about computers,' he said. 'I leave that to my secretary. Or I would if I had one. The previous girl left a couple of months ago and we haven't replaced her yet. We've tried temps, but Anny hasn't been happy with any of them. Here's the wild animal pavilion. Elizabeth's still here, waiting for her passport to Italy. I'll introduce you.'

Elizabeth seemed to recognize him. She trotted over and he hunkered down and sweet-talked her through the bars. He seemed to find it easier to chat up wolves than women. But his welcoming smile had been very warm. I got down beside him and resisted the temptation to put my fingers through the bars of the cage.

'So you don't have any records left at all, anywhere? Surely Monsieur Andrieu kept copies?'

'Not a thing,' he said simply. 'He was very upset about it all. Nothing's left.'

'Anny said last night that the alarm didn't go off.'

'There was an electrical fault. The concierge, Monsieur Paul, is here during the day, and when he leaves, he switches on the alarm system. On this occasion, it seems there was a short-circuit and the alarm didn't go on.'

'That's a bit of a coincidence,' I murmured, watching his profile.

'The security company thought the fault might have been intermittent.' His attention was still on the beautiful animal in the cage. 'I don't know much about that sort of thing. But they tell me the new system's more reliable. And we're going to get a night concierge too.'

'I'm surprised you didn't have one before. Who looks

after the animals if something happens at night?'

'Up till now, no one. I was amazed when I learned about it too, but Monsieur Andrieu was anxious to keep costs down. Anyway, now he's agreed, and we're advertising the post.'

'Didn't the previous director find it odd?' I asked, getting up to ease my aching knees. Jean-Loup glanced up at me with a look of surprise. 'The previous director was Monsieur Andrieu himself,' he explained. 'But it got too much for him, with all his other interests. That's why he hired me.'

A voice said angrily: 'Oh, there you are, Jean-Loup. I've been looking for you everywhere. You're wanted on the phone.'

It was Anny Baeke, dressed in worn jeans and a faded T-shirt with damp patches under the arms. She was looking harassed and irritable. Jean-Loup got to his feet, said: 'Excuse me,' and hurried out. Anny cast a fierce look at me and followed him. You didn't need to be Hercule Poirot to see she didn't like me.

I wandered round for a while on my own, but to tell the truth, the sight of animals doing time always saddens me, so I left the animal houses and went out into the sunshine again. Byron T. was sitting on a bench eating an ice-cream, next to a small bright stall selling refreshments. As I went over, he rose in haste and dropped the remainder of the ice-cream on his trousers. 'Where's Edward?' I asked, as he scrubbed away with his hanky.

'Inside. He told me to wait here.' He looked round for somewhere to put the sticky hanky and ended up putting it into his pocket.

'Poor old Byron T.,' I said. 'You have a lot to put up with, don't you?'

He looked up at me with a luminous smile. 'Oh no, ma'am. It's all wonderful. And when the conference is over, I can get down to some real stuff. I want to go

54

to the Congo Museum, and find out all about King Leopold and Henry M. Stanley. Henry M. Stanley's my hero. He was American, you know. I had so much fun in London tracking him down – and your Dr Livingstone too. They were really great men.'

Hero-worship shone out of the blue eyes, and I had to smile. There was a genuine, boyish enthusiasm about Byron T.

'So you want to track him down here too?' I said. 'Well, there's a bit about him in the museum, but you might find more in the Albertine – the Royal Library. They're bound to have all the information about King Leopold's dealings with Stanley.'

'Will you take me there? To help with the language and so on. I'd really appreciate it.'

I couldn't say no. 'OK. When the conference is finished we'll go and do all that.'

'I can't wait,' he said, beaming.

We all drove home in moderate harmony. The street was sunny and quiet as I pulled in and parked opposite my front door. Edward and Byron T. got out and made to cross the road. Edward hadn't locked his door. Grumbling, I leaned over to push the lock down. Through my open window, I heard a sudden ominous crash of gears and the revving of heavy engines. I jerked my head round, vertebrae cracking, to see a huge, filthy truck roaring down the narrow road behind us, travelling far too fast. Edward and Byron T. were frozen in the middle of the road. I screamed a warning, scrabbling uselessly for the door-handle. The truck thundered past in a cloud of dirt, its wheels half on the pavement outside my door, and disappeared off up the road. As I scrambled frantically out of the car, I saw Byron T. and Edward pressed up against the wall of my house. Byron T. had his arm across Edward. They seemed to be unhurt. I charged across.

'By Jove,' Edward said shakily, 'that was a narrow

squeak. Nearly drove over my feet. But thanks to Byron, it's no worse. Thank you, my boy. You were very quick.'

'Glad to be of help, sir. But was that close! Did you see who it was, Matilda?'

I'd had a brief glimpse of a filthy windscreen, the interior obscured by a forest of dangling furry animals and other modern fetishes.

'There wasn't time,' I said, 'and the number plates were so covered with dirt I couldn't make them out.'

We were all beginning to shake. Byron T. looked at us. 'It seems like accidents follow you around, Dr Haycastle.' Then he added gently: 'Or maybe it was no accident?'

'I don't think we'll ever know,' said Edward. 'Matilda, can we go inside? I feel rather conspicuous standing here on the doorstep.'

As I put the key in the front door, I became aware that a strange sound was coming out of the house. As the door opened, I identified it: Arab pop music. With it came wafting the rich, spicy smell of couscous. Yasmina appeared from the kitchen with a huge apron on, a large spoon in her hand, and a wide smile on her face.

'Surprise!' said Edward. 'I thought I'd save you the bother of cooking tonight.'

He and Yasmina had planned it between them – a real couscous, chickpeas and all. Yasmina had spent all day preparing it. Real couscous needs steaming for ten hours, but her grandmother had helped. She'd made two lots – vegetable for Edward and herself, mutton for Byron T. and me. There were dishes full of green and red things floating in oil, bottles of suspicious-looking brown stuff and a large pot of the dreaded *harissa*. There were six bottles of Beaujolais – Edward had drawn the line at North African wine. It was a feast. Recovering from our shock, and perhaps suffering slightly from over-reaction, we laughed, joked and stuffed ourselves silly. Byron T. retired early, no doubt from the effects of couscous and pizza combined, but Edward and Yasmina and I sat talking over the wine till long after midnight. At least, he and Yasmina talked. I watched them and thought about road accidents.

Chapter 8

Bad news greeted us the following morning. Byron T. had been struck down overnight by an excess of exotic food. There would be no American pancakes for breakfast today.

'Dehaene's revenge,' said Edward unsympathetically. 'I told him he shouldn't have eaten those peppers. But he says he'll try and come down this afternoon for my speech if he's feeling better.'

'Have you changed the speech at all?' I enquired.

Edward shook his head decisively. 'Certainly not.'

'What about last night's little warning? If that was an accident, I'm Bambi's mother. Andrieu *must* be on to you.'

'If he thinks I'm giving in to that kind of blackmail, he's mistaken,' Edward said. 'We'll just have to keep our eyes open.'

He stopped, cast me a quick glance then said cajolingly: 'Matilda?'

I knew that tone.

'How long?' I asked, resigned.

Edward looked startled. 'What?'

'How long do you want to stay on after the conference?'

'How on earth did you know I was going to ask that?'

'I'm a mind-reader. How long?'

'However long it takes. But I can send Byron home if you prefer.'

58

'Don't do that,' I said. 'He's got to do his research on Henry M. Stanley. Anyway, I'm getting used to having him around. I haven't washed up since he arrived.'

'I must admit I'm rather fond of the boy too. He saved my life out there last night, you know. The old reactions are slowing down, but he got me out of the way just in time. So you don't mind?'

'Not a bit. Byron stays too. I've got a few ideas on how we can proceed. I'll find out all I can about Andrieu's business interests. And there's the Wolfman angle to pursue.'

Edward gave me a shrewd look. 'I get the feeling that you have a personal interest in that particular aspect of the affair.'

I kept my face straight. 'I like tall men,' I said.

'Well, don't get too attached. It's possible he may be in on anything nefarious that's going on. After all, he works for Andrieu.'

It was only common sense to consider it, but I have to admit I felt a slight chill at the possibility. I made a mental note to call Paris as soon as possible. It was important to me to know that Jean-Loup was in the clear.

'Incidentally, whatever happened to that policeman you were running around with?' Edward seemed unwilling to drop the subject of my sex-life. 'You should have heard your mother about that one.'

'I did. He went to the US. We don't write.' I hoped my tone would have a discouraging effect. My uncle gave me another thoughtful look, but didn't pursue the subject.

I was already sick of the sight of the Burgundia, and there was still a day and a half to go. The number of delegates had thinned out – fine weather and the sights of Brussels were proving more attractive than sitting in an air-conditioned conference room. Andrieu also was conspicuous by his absence. I slept peacefully in my chair till the mid-morning break. It took two large cups of coffee to revive me. I was downing the third when one of the cerise girls touched my sleeve. It was the pretty one, as painted as a geisha. There was a phone call for me. I went to the foyer and was directed to a small plush booth. At the other end of the line was Byron T.

'Matilda? I'm feeling better now, so I figured I'd come on out. Can you give me directions on how to get there? I should make it by lunchtime.'

I sighed. Surely he could have asked the receptionist instead of disturbing me? 'Take a taxi,' I said. I gave him the number to call and all the relevant coordinates, and he thanked me and rang off. I stared at the phone. Since I was here, I might as well check out Jean-Loup. I knew the name of his previous employers so I called Directory Enquiries and got the number. A moment later, I was speaking to Jean-Loup's ex-secretary. A chatty lady. She supplied me with all the details about his old job, his new job, and even gave me his address and phone number in Belgium. He'd worked in his previous job for five years and had been made redundant after a company merger. He'd taken the Belgian job because it was the only one he'd applied for that had come up, though he'd really hoped to be able to stay on in France. It sounded very convincing, I thought as I put the phone down, though a small voice in the back of my mind was wondering if I wasn't rather too ready to be convinced.

As I emerged from the booth, Monique Ryckmans came by, immaculate in a lime green suit. She gave me a long, level look as she passed. For my money, she was the most dangerous element in the whole damn mess.

My cheerfulness soon evaporated. I'd lost Edward again. But this time the cerise dollies had seen him:

going down in the lift to the car park. I couldn't believe my ears. What was this, some kind of obsession? For the second time in three days, I rocketed down the stairs and emerged panting into the basement area. Edward was standing over by some dustbins, apparently waiting. 'What on earth are you doing?' I yelled.

He swung round startled as I raced over and made a gesture as if to say 'Get away!' At the same moment there was a dull crack and something whistled past my ear and smacked into the scenery behind me. Before I knew where I was, I found myself flat on the ground with Edward's arm holding me down.

'What the hell was that?' I got out, shocked, but I knew what it was all right. I'd heard that sound too often in films.

'Somebody took a shot at us,' said Edward in my ear, rather calmly under the circumstances. 'Keep your head down and don't move.'

My face was practically in a puddle of oil and I could smell the ripeness of the huge garbage bins behind us. Then there was a loud ting, and the lift doors opened to disgorge a party of people who dispersed to their cars, laughing and talking.

'Quick,' said Edward. Heads turned as he pulled me to my feet and dragged me by the hand across the car park to the lift. A moment later we were in the safety of the warmth and bright lights again. There was dirt all over my skirt. I turned to Edward and saw that he was ghastly white and trembling with shock. I wasn't feeling all that perky myself. I put an arm round him and we stumbled out of the lift together.

'Don't say anything,' I muttered. 'Come and sit down.'

I helped him along the corridor to the coffee area, got him into a chair and sent the cerise dolly for a brandy.

'What were you doing down there? Edward, what's going on?'

He lifted a hand: 'Better in a minute. Got a fright. Give me a minute.'

The geisha came fluttering back, wide-eyed, and between us we poured the brandy into Edward. He started to look a bit more like himself, enough to give the girl a smile and reassure her.

'Nice little popsy,' he murmured, as she tripped back to her desk.

'What's going on?' I demanded resolutely, and for answer, he reached into a pocket and handed me a folded open envelope with the Burgundia logo on it. Inside was a sheet of A4 paper with the Burgundia letterhead, and a printed paragraph:

I believe it is necessary that we should resolve our differences without further delay. I suggest we find some private venue and will await you at my car at 10.45 (basement garage).
PMA

'And you went?' I asked incredulously.

'Of course. I thought we were getting somewhere at last. But there was nobody there. And then you turned up.' Edward's eyes narrowed. 'So much for the gun being stolen. By God, it's just the kind of trick that scoundrel would play.'

'First the truck and now this,' I said. 'You've got to tell the police.'

He uttered a short laugh. 'What for? We won't be able to prove anything.'

'There might be fingerprints on the letter.'

Edward stared at me. 'But then they'll find out about the car.'

'If this ridiculous feud goes on, you're going to end up dead,' I said. 'And how am I going to explain that to Inspector Guillaume? You've got to come clean.'

'Not yet, Matilda. Please. Just give it a few more days. Otherwise Andrieu will get away with it again. Believe me, I know how he operates.'

'Then you were daft to go down there,' I said, but I could see Edward wasn't listening.

'I'm amazed he'd be stupid enough to try anything in such a public place,' he mused, eyes half-closed. 'He must really be getting rattled. Good, we're obviously barking up the right tree. Just a few more days, my darling niece. Please.'

'All right,' I agreed, reluctantly. 'But for heaven's sake, try and be sensible. By the way, Byron's feeling better. He's coming out for lunch.'

'You'll have him all to yourself then,' Edward said. 'I'm lunching with Ilse.'

I groaned. 'Do me a favour – keep a low profile.'

I might as well have asked King Kong to keep a low profile. At the end of the morning session we broke for lunch. Sitting at a small table in the café, I saw Edward and Ilse, his hand discreetly on her arm, heading for the more expensive restaurant. She was looking up at him in a way that gave me a twinge of unease. It could only be described as adoring. They sat down where I could see them, just inside the door. I turned back, frowning, and picked up the menu. As I did so, a flash of lime green caught my eye, and I realized that Andrieu and Monique Ryckmans were sitting not ten metres from me. They'd obviously seen Edward and Ilse too. Andrieu was staring over his shoulder at them. I couldn't see his face, but I could see hers all right. She was looking at me, and her expression was like Hortense's when she's bird-watching.

Thankfully I was rescued from a potentially awkward situation by the arrival of Byron T., completely recovered, enthusiasm undimmed. He'd had an adventure with the taxi, which he told me all about at length. He and the taxi-driver had been unable to find a mutually comprehensible means of communication, and they'd ended up hopelessly lost on the wrong side of town, finally driving the wrong way down a one-way street and getting stuck in a pot-hole, right in the path of an approaching tram. There had then been an altercation with the tram-driver, who had become abusive, and then some of the passengers had got involved, and the tram-driver had called in reinforcements over his radio. It could only have happened to Byron T.

As this epic came mercifully to its end, Andrieu and Monique Ryckmans rose and left together. I watched them go, then re-focused on Byron T., who was now gassing on about Stanley and Livingstone. His view of African exploration was irredeemably Disneyish – clean, sporting and full of gentlemanly bonhomie, a sort of early Cook's Tour to the sources of the Nile. In his eyes, Stanley could do no wrong. I thought of Queen Victoria writing to King Leopold to warn him about Stanley's reputation for brutality. I thought of Leopold and Stanley sitting down with a map of Africa between them and carefully marking out with a red pencil the bit they were going to grab. But I kept my mouth shut.

Having exhausted Africa, Byron T. passed on to American football, nattering happily and apparently not noticing how uncommunicative I was. But as I called for the bill, he put a large hand on my arm.

'I don't mean to pry, Matilda, but is everything OK? You seem really quiet, like there was something wrong.'

'No, I'm fine,' I replied. 'A little shaken by last night, that's all.'

'Well, if there's anything I can do for you, let me know. I'd be only too pleased.'

I couldn't help but be touched, and for a moment was tempted to confide. But then I reconsidered. The fewer people who knew about this sorry mess, the better.

Ten minutes' walk alone in the fresh air prepared me for the afternoon's proceedings. As I resumed my seat, I caught sight of Edward near the platform, talking to Ilse Müller. They were gesticulating. They seemed agitated. As I watched, he turned abruptly and hurried off through a side-door behind the platform. Ilse took a step after him, her hand out as if to stop him. Now what? I made my way down the aisle as quickly as I could without arousing undue attention. Ilse was wringing her hands.

'What's happening?' I asked. 'Where's Edward gone?'

'Oh, Miss Haycastle – this is terrible. I have to do my duty, he must understand that. I have to do as Mr Andrieu says.'

'But what did he say?' I asked impatiently.

'It's all so unfortunate, but I can do nothing. He will not be speaking today. Mr Andrieu feels that there are parts of the speech that are rather too ... inflammatory. It is all most embarrassing. He instructed me to tell Dr Haycastle that the speech is cancelled.'

'Where's Edward gone?' I repeated, interrupting.

'To find Mr Andrieu, but he seemed so angry – I am afraid he will do something ...'

'Where? Quick, tell me.'

'Madame Ryckmans's office. Through there, up the stairs and to the right.'

I shot out of the door like Linford Christie, galloped up the stairs, and skidded to a halt. There were four wooden doors. I tried them all. A stationery cupboard. A photocopying room. An office with a startled girl in it. I muttered an apology and was opening the fourth door when I heard Ilse's breathless voice behind me.

'No, no, no. Not there. Around the corner.'

Round the corner was a half-open door. Ilse panted up behind me as I got there, just in time to hear

Edward say, with disastrous clarity: 'If you do that, I swear I'll kill you.'

I heard Ilse gasp. I pushed the door open and saw them standing square on to each other, as if they were about to come to blows. My uncle was leaning forward slightly, his hands clenched. I couldn't see his face, but I could see Andrieu's. It was full of hate. Then he caught sight of Ilse and me gaping in the doorway and his expression changed. My uncle, too, turned and saw us. He was white, but seemed to be in control of himself.

'Matilda,' he said. 'My dear. I've had enough of this. We're leaving.'

He said nothing at all as we went back to the conference room, gathered our possessions, collected a bewildered Byron T. and left. But as soon as we reached the avenue de Tervueren, Edward asked to be let out of the car.

'I need to walk,' he said. 'To think. You two go off home. Don't worry about me. I'll get home on my own.'

It was the last thing I wanted him to do, but I couldn't very well stop him. I made sure he had the spare keys, my phone number and address, and dropped him, as he asked, at the entrance to the Cinquantenaire park.

'I may be late,' was all he said. Byron T. and I watched him walk away swiftly, hands in pockets, head bent. I was preparing to drive off when I heard the door slam and became aware that Byron T. had leapt out too.

'What the heck are you doing?' I demanded, staring.

'He shouldn't be left alone,' said Byron T. determinedly. 'I'm going to follow him. You just go home and don't worry. Nothing'll happen to him while I'm around.'

And with that, he was off like a rabbit into the

throng of tourists and women with push-chairs. They were both as mad as hatters. I looked at my watch: nearly three. I'd had enough. I was going home.

Back at the flat I lay down for a nap, dreamt that somebody had cut off all Hortense's paws, and woke up sweating and anguished to the sound of someone knocking on the door. Staggering down disoriented and dishevelled, I found Byron T. on the doorstep.

'Is he back?' he asked instantly. 'I lost him.'

I shook my head. 'Come on in. There's nothing more we can do. He'll come home when he's ready.'

It was seven o'clock. Pulling myself together, I cooked some dinner and we ate. Byron T. made huge, kind efforts to distract me, and spent the meal leaping up and down fetching dishes, pouring wine, making coffee and, finally, washing up. He couldn't have been sweeter, but all this worry was wearing me out. By nine, I could hardly keep my eyes open. I muttered an excuse and headed for the stairs.

'Is it OK if I watch some TV?' I heard Byron T. call after me. A moment later, I heard the sound of canned laughter coming up faintly through the floorboards. That was the last thing I remember.

Chapter 9

We were woken up next day by someone knocking on the door. I thought I was dreaming at first, but it persisted. I opened bleary eyes and realized someone wanted to come in. Edward, I thought confusedly, but no, he had the spare keys. And what time was it anyway? I hauled my weary limbs from the bed, peered out of the window and saw a police van, pulled up illegally on the pavement.

Oh Christ, he's had an accident, was my first thought. Galvanized, I tumbled down the stairs and unlocked the front door, pulling my dressing-gown round me. Outside was the cadaverous form and prominent nose of Inspector Guillaume. Not exactly what you want to find on your doorstep on a sunny Sunday morning.

'What's happened?' I demanded. 'Where's my uncle?'

He looked at me with astonishment, his mouth clamped tight.

'That's what I wanted to ask you.'

Behind me, a voice said: 'Matilda, what is it?' and there was Edward, clad in dark blue Marks & Spencer pyjamas. Relief weakened my knees. Across the street, curtains twitched. A car drove by, slowing down to take in the exciting view. I stepped back and said: 'Come in.'

Behind Edward, Byron T. was hovering on the stairs. Engagingly, his pyjamas had Playboy rabbits all over them. Guillaume was in the same raincoat as before. I wondered if he ever took it off.

Leading the way through to the living room, I pulled myself together and asked: 'What can we do for you?'

Guillaume was looking round with the air of a social-ist who finds himself obliged to breathe bourgeois air against his will. 'Very nice,' he said sneeringly. 'Very nice indeed. Cost a pretty penny, I expect.'

'I wouldn't know,' I replied. 'I rent it.'

'Ah yes,' he said. 'From a friend. You have a lot of friends, don't you?'

He made the word 'friend' sound dirty. What was all this? I wished I were feeling a little more lively. Witty repartee was a touch beyond me at the moment.

He went to the front window and stood looking out, while we waited like lemons. Then he said abruptly, switching languages to English: 'Where were you all last night? You, Miss Haycastle?'

'Here, in bed.'

'Can you prove it?'

I turned to Byron T., who said: 'I can vouch for it. We were here together.'

'Together?' Guillaume pounced instantly on the word.

Byron T. went bright red. With considerable dignity, he explained: 'We had supper, then Miss Haycastle went upstairs to her room around nine o'clock. I watched television till midnight and then I went to bed also. In my room.'

'Of course. And Dr Haycastle?'

I looked at Edward's face, which was tired and lined.

'I was out till the early hours,' he said. 'I got back here around three o'clock. They were both asleep. I let myself in.'

'Did either of you hear him?' Guillaume asked us.

Byron T. looked at me, then at Guillaume and shook his head.

'No,' I said.

'And where were you until three o'clock?'

'Wandering. I walked round the parks, then I had a meal, went to the Grand'Place, sat in a café for a while and walked home.'

'You *walked* from the Grand'Place to Boitsfort?' Guillaume repeated, raising a ragged eyebrow. 'How long did it take you?'

'A couple of hours. Maybe more.'

'Why not take a taxi?'

'I needed the exercise,' said Edward. 'And I wanted to think.'

'Dr Haycastle, when did you last see Philippe Andrieu? The exact time please.'

'Just after two o'clock yesterday afternoon.' said Edward frowning. 'At the Burgundia.'

Byron T. and I both confirmed this. I was starting to have a nasty feeling. I'd been down this road before.

There was a silence. Then Guillaume said: 'I want this house searched. I have a warrant.'

I couldn't believe my ears. 'What for?' I demanded, stepping forward. 'What are you looking for?'

'A gun.' Guillaume's tone was nonchalant. 'The gun that killed Philippe Andrieu last night.'

I suppose policemen like being dramatic. One of the perks of the job.

The three of us sat silently in the kitchen while the police searched the house. Hortense had taken refuge in the loo cupboard again. I'd suddenly remembered the papers Edward had nicked from Andrieu's car, and was feeling rather sick. I looked at my uncle who smiled and patted my knee. He couldn't say anything because Guillaume was with us, but I felt slightly reassured.

They didn't find anything. They let us dress, escorted us to a police station and took statements. Byron T. and I sat side by side in uncomfortable chairs for half an hour while Edward was grilled. Then I sat alone for a further half-hour while Byron T. was grilled. Then it was my turn.

'This isn't the first time the police have had the pleasure of dealing with you, Miss Haycastle,' was Guillaume's first comment. 'You seem to pop up quite regularly in our files. All that unsavoury business with the lamented ex-Inspector Vanderauwera and then the Gheyssens affair. We've got a nice little dossier on you.'

He leaned back in his chair and surveyed me.

'And what's Vanderauwera up to these days?' he asked. 'Something dubious, no doubt.'

Not for the first time, I reflected that my affair with Luc Vanderauwera was going to haunt me for the rest of my life.

'I haven't the slightest idea,' I said wearily. 'If you want to know, I can give you his mother's phone number.'

'Moved on, eh?' Guillaume said, with that nasty insinuating inflection.

'What's it to you?' I said. 'It's got nothing to do with anything. If you've got something to ask me, ask. Then we can all go home.'

For the first time, there was a change in his expression, as if he'd found something he hadn't expected. I wished my brain wasn't quite so woolly. The strain had been more telling than I thought.

Then quite abruptly, Guillaume said: 'There was some kind of grievance between your uncle and Philippe Andrieu. Do you know what it was?'

It was time to tell the truth. Some of it, anyway.

'They fell out in the Congo, years ago,' I said. 'A quarrel over a girl. And later, in Kenya, Edward found out that Andrieu was involved in poaching activities.'

'Did he have any proof?'

'Nothing concrete.'

'And has he seen Andrieu since then? Until the conference?'

'I don't know.'

'But there have been at least two disputes between them during the conference. What were these about?'

'Andrieu wanted him to make some changes to one of his speeches. Edward considered it to be censorship.'

'I've been told that your uncle accused Andrieu, before witnesses, of being a murderer. Why should he do that?'

'He thinks Andrieu was responsible for the death of one of his friends in Kenya.'

'A close friend?'

'I think so.'

'Do you think he is the kind of man who might plan revenge?' Guillaume asked softly.

I remembered the look on Edward's face when he'd told me about his friend's death, and I wasn't at all sure.

'I don't know,' I said again.

'He has no alibi,' Guillaume went on in the same soft tone. 'Interesting, don't you think?'

There wasn't any more I could tell him, so he let me go. I stopped in the corridor, wondering why I was feeling so dozy. I'd fudged the issue of whether or not Edward was capable of revenge. He'd told me it was justice he wanted, but how did I know that was true? I hardly knew him at all.

Chapter 10

'Of course I didn't bloody do it,' Edward said irritably. 'This is a damned nuisance. Now I'll never get the information I need and Byron and I are stuck in this bloody country till they get the mess sorted out.'

'Never mind that,' I said, just as irritably. 'Don't you realize that a) you haven't got an alibi and b) you have, unfortunately, got a motive?'

'They haven't any proof,' bellowed my uncle. 'Where's the weapon? Where are the witnesses? You can't arrest somebody on suspicion.'

'This is Belgium,' I said. We stared at one another for a moment.

'Well, what would a Belgian do?' demanded Edward.

That was easy: 'Get a lawyer.'

Edward didn't give in easily, but I got my way in the end – by threatening to blow the gaff if he didn't agree. I don't know if I'd have actually been able to do it, but luckily Edward thought I would.

I had the name of a lawyer, provided by my oldest Belgian friend Georges Duchanel, in case, he said, of necessity. He'd added a few pithy comments about some people perhaps finding it more necessary than others, but I'd ignored those. I'd never used the lawyer either, but this was definitely an emergency.

Georges wasn't in Belgium at the moment. He was on a six-month cruise, because of his heart. His problems were not, however, medical. Madeleine, his elegant, well-bred mistress, had left him.

'She had a better offer,' Georges had said over the phone, with profound but theatrical melancholy, when announcing his departure. 'Marriage. To a man who collects tropical fish. They sent me an invitation to the wedding. Kind of them, don't you think, but it would have seemed too much like a funeral, so I did not go. I shall remove myself to more temperate climes and repair my shattered emotions.'

So Georges was repairing his shattered emotions somewhere in the South Seas, and I was stuck with a lunatic uncle, a grown-up boy-scout and a murder.

I called the lawyer first thing Monday. His name was Richard Grandville and his office was in the avenue de Tervueren. The secretary offered me an appointment next week, so I mentioned Georges's name and she suggested that afternoon. At two-thirty Edward and I were sitting in front of a slight, dark-haired man with an intelligent face and mild blue eyes. He spoke perfect English with no trace of accent. I had heard him speak equally perfect French to his secretary. He sat back in his chair, a gold fountain-pen in his fingers, and listened as I gave a brief run-down of the problem. When I finished, he was silent for a moment, then said: 'I should like to talk to you alone, Dr Haycastle. Miss Haycastle, would you mind waiting outside?'

I waited outside, with a cup of coffee provided by the efficient, polite secretary, and a copy of *The Economist*. I have often had cause to admire the talent of *The Economist*'s headline writers, but today they couldn't compete for my attention. It seemed like a million years before the door opened and my uncle came out. He looked disgruntled.

'He wants you now,' he said.

I went in. Grandville was in his chair, looking out of the window, his back to me.

'What was the cause of that last argument?' he said abruptly. 'When he threatened Andrieu.'

'I don't know. I only heard the very last part of it.'

'Can you remember exactly?'

I hesitated. But I had to tell the truth to my lawyer or there wasn't any point in having one. I took a deep breath. 'I heard my uncle say: "You do that and I swear I'll kill you".'

'Is that all?' said the back of the chair.

'That's all I heard.'

'Do you know what he was referring to?'

'No. It sounded as if Andrieu had made some sort of threat. But it must have been something very serious. Edward sounded as if he really meant it.'

There was a silence, then suddenly the chair swung round again. The blue eyes took me in from head to foot – they didn't seem quite as mild as before. Grandville looked down at the very expensive blotter on his desk. 'Did anyone else hear it?' he asked.

'Yes. Ilse Müller was there. Andrieu's secretary. And I think she must have told the police.'

'That's a pity.'

'That's an understatement,' I replied, somewhat grimly. 'He's got a glaring motive and he hasn't got an alibi.'

'Do you think he killed Andrieu?' asked Grandville gently, watching me.

'No,' I said. 'Edward wanted him exposed as a crook. He wanted to prove him guilty and bring him to justice. And we're talking about a man who hates the thought of taking any kind of life.' It crossed my mind that Edward might possibly have made an exception for Andrieu, but I suppressed the thought. Grandville must have read it on my face, however, because he said softly: 'You're not sure?'

'He says he didn't and I believe him,' I said stoutly. 'There are half a dozen people involved in this who might have done it. Maybe he'd fallen out with Monique Ryckmans. Maybe Ilse Müller went off her head and did it. Maybe it had nothing to do with any of us. And anyway, if what Edward's told me is true, Andrieu had it coming.'

'The police are unlikely to be impressed by that,' Grandville observed with a slight grimace. 'I have to tell you, Miss Haycastle, that I felt your uncle was being less than frank about the subject of that last quarrel. You must realize that it's a crucial piece of evidence. It could be the motive for murder.'

I felt very cold all of a sudden, and then very hot.

'Furthermore,' Grandville went on, 'I can't emphasize sufficiently how foolish your uncle has been in not telling the police about the car break-in. Doing it in the first place was an act of utter stupidity, but keeping it from the police will only make the situation worse.'

'My words almost exactly,' I said, 'but he's absolutely adamant. What do you want me to do? Denounce him?'

'You could be accused of complicity,' he said gently. 'Not to mention perverting the course of justice. The sooner your uncle tells the truth, the better for you both.'

'I'll just have to get used to picking oakum,' I said ruefully.

'Pardon me?'

'Nothing. Listen, I shall quite understand if you don't want to take us on. But I really don't think Edward killed anybody, and I intend to do everything I can to prove it.'

There was another pause, during which I reflected that there was no reason on earth why he'd want anything to do with us. Then: 'What made you think I didn't want to take it on?' Grandville enquired mildly. 'I'll do anything I can to help. But there's one condition.'

'Name it,' I said.

'Don't do anything illegal. Things are complicated enough as they are.'

'OK.'

'I have my sources in the police,' he went on, 'and I'll find out as much as I can about the circumstances of the murder. From what you say, your uncle may well be the main suspect, but if the police had any real proof, they'd have arrested him by now. I'll be in touch. Do what you can, but stay out of trouble.'

The trouble is, I've always found that easier said than done.

Chapter 11

Ilse Müller was first on my list. I had an argument with Edward about who was going to talk to her, which I won, and at nine o'clock the next morning I was outside her front door. I'd rung up and given her a whole spiel about how Edward needed her help, and the charm must still have been working because she sounded positively eager to talk to me. But perhaps she was just keen to see a friendly face.

She had a small, cluttered apartment on the ground floor of a dingy block in Etterbeek. It was rather dim inside, with faded carpets and curtains, brownish cotton print shawls draped over the chairs, neglected plants in macramé holders and a general air of muddle. Ilse was looking terrible and seemed on edge. I suppose it's not every day your boss gets murdered, though some secretaries might consider it wish-fulfilment.

Not Ilse. I had to listen to ten minutes' solid anguish before I could get my first question in. She'd worked for Andrieu for fifteen years and she was fifty-two years old and how was she ever going to find another job at her age, and with the same salary, and she'd probably have to go home to Germany now and it had all changed so much since the wall came down and she'd have to live with her mother in Frankfurt and all her old friends were dead or had moved away.

She spoke in a fast, brittle, high-pitched voice. I wondered briefly if she was taking any kind of medication. She was chain-smoking too – the apartment reeked of stale smoke and there were full ashtrays in the living room. Her hair looked dead and stringy.

I soothed, reassured and suggested that a cup of something might help, then regretted it when Ilse made a pot of herbal tea which tasted like horse-liniment. I explained Edward's predicament all over again, which provoked a storm of self-flagellation. It had all been Ilse's fault. Mr Andrieu had been angry when he saw her having lunch with Edward, and that was probably why he'd been so unpleasant about Edward's speech. If only Ilse hadn't said anything, none of it would have happened. Edward had been so good to her, and she'd only made things worse. Nobody had ever treated her with such consideration as Edward. No man, that is. Tears came into her eyes as she said it, and I murmured soothingly and patted her shoulder.

A little silence fell. Carefully, I asked Ilse how she'd got on with Andrieu. Had he been a good boss? She gave me a quick, rather frightened look and then rattled off again, so fast I had trouble following her words.

He'd been a very difficult man to get to know, though of course after fifteen years you do get used to somebody's little ways, and no, she hadn't found him too difficult though he was sometimes rather out of temper and such a stickler about privacy and confidentiality, and he'd told her off really nastily once because she'd forgotten to password-protect a couple of really unimportant documents on the word processor, but no boss was really perfect, was he, so one just had to put up with what one couldn't change. Didn't one? Again, the frightened flickering glance.

'Yes,' I said. 'Was he married?'

He was divorced, five years ago, and such a nice woman his wife had been, but then that appalling Monique Ryckmans had got her hooks into him and really, the way they were carrying on at the dinner the other night was an absolute disgrace. Still (this with venomous satisfaction), Monique wouldn't get her hands on the money now. She couldn't persuade him to marry her and now it was too late.

'What money?' I asked.

Well, everybody knew that Mr Andrieu had made an absolute fortune out of the family mining enterprise in the Congo and, of course, it had all been invested. There was a considerable sum in a Swiss bank, plus business interests in Belgium and all over the world, and a house in Provence and another in the Swiss Alps.

'Who's going to get the money?' I enquired, heroically accepting another cup of horse-liniment. 'Are there any kids?'

No children of his own, and no relatives. Ilse had always understood that the money was to be left in trust to support the various charities that Andrieu was involved in, but only his lawyer had those details. Of course, the government would get most of it, which was a dreadful shame.

'What are his business interests in Belgium?' I asked. 'Do you have a list?'

Yes, but it was in the office, and do you know what they'd done? His lawyer had told her that her services were no longer needed and she'd had to leave her work just as it was, with a letter half-typed on the machine. They hadn't even let her collect her own personal belongings and there was a little vase her mother had given her and a packet of biscuits and some aspirins still in her desk drawer.

I tried to get her to remember as many of the Belgian business interests as she could. There was the Burgundia, of course, Les Fauves, and a small transcontinental courier service based out at Zaventem.

'Name?' I asked, scribbling.

'PA Express.'

'What about the rest of the world?'

She couldn't help me with that, because she had handled only part of his affairs – the rest was taken care of by Madame Greenberg.

The question written on my face must have been: 'Who on earth is Madame Greenberg?'

She was the secretary at Les Fauves – at least, she had been, but she'd left rather suddenly a few weeks ago. She'd been working with Andrieu for years and years too, then they'd fallen out over something and she'd resigned. There had been a series of temps since then, and everything was in a shocking mess because, as everybody knows, most temps are just not efficient, are they?

I ignored that, and asked if she knew where we could contact Madame Greenberg. But it was impossible, she'd left Brussels with no forwarding address and anyway, Anita Greenberg was the sort of person who wouldn't tell anybody anything unless she had a gun held to her head. A real oyster, said Ilse. She seemed more cheerful: the therapeutic effects of confession. Would I like another cup of camomile tea?

By the way, I asked, as she was seeing me out, where was she on Saturday night? There was no hesitation. She'd been out at a discotheque with her Singles Club. I couldn't imagine Ilse bopping till dawn in some night-spot, but perhaps I was just an old fogey.

I left with my insides awash and my head ringing.

Byron T. had taken like a man the news that he couldn't leave the country, and with unwonted tact had announced that he would take the opportunity to get on with his research. That meant he would be out from under our feet all day, which eased our guilt at not telling him anything. He wasn't back when I got home, so I was able to fill Edward in immediately. He heard me out with a frown and then said:

81

'Well, what now?'

'Les Fauves. I'm going to volunteer my services as a temporary helper.'

'You watch out.' Edward grinned unexpectedly. 'You'll end up mucking out elephants.'

'They haven't got any elephants,' I said with dignity. 'And after living with Hortense, elephants would be light relief. I'll also get down to the *Moniteur Belge* offices to try and find out more about Andrieu's business interests.'

'I could check out this courier firm,' Edward said. Seeing the word No on my lips, he added: 'I can do that on the phone, without moving from the house. Come on, Matilda, I can't just sit here doing nothing while you charge round town like a cut-price version of *Charlie's Angels*.'

Cut price? Bloody cheek.

'What about you?' I said crossly. 'If you hadn't been behaving like some sexagenarian Indiana Jones, we wouldn't have got into this mess in the first place.'

'Who's Indiana Jones?' asked my uncle.

Chapter 12

I called Jean-Loup and offered my services for that afternoon. The offer was accepted with flattering alacrity, but when I got to Les Fauves, I discovered that Jean-Loup had been called away to Brussels for a meeting with Andrieu's lawyers. He would be back in the late afternoon. In the meantime I found myself, somewhat to my discomfort, in the hands of Anny Baeke.

'Oh,' she said, looking at me doubtfully with those china-blue eyes. 'It's quite hard work, you know. And rather messy. Are you sure you'll be able to manage?'

'I hope so.' I smiled sweetly at her, wondering if I sounded as insincere as I felt.

One's sins always find one out. My insincerity was amply repaid. In the next three hours, I humped bales of straw, swept out pens, scrubbed cages with disinfectant and heaved boxes of feed around like a navvy. I was on my own. Anny hadn't bothered to introduce me to the other staff. Monsieur Paul, the concierge, had recognized me when I came in, and had waved and smiled. I'd also caught a glimpse of a couple of white-coated men working in what seemed to be a surgery, but apart from that, the shelter was very quiet.

By about four o'clock, I was beginning to realize that it was no coincidence I was getting all the dirty jobs. Ms Baeke was doing it on purpose. I was starting to get tired, and my back was aching from the bending down. I'd broken two fingernails, ripped the sleeve of my shirt on a cage door and pulled a long thread out of my new trousers. As I finished the last cage, straightening up with a weary sigh, the door opened and Monsieur Paul came in with some odds and ends.

'You're working hard,' he remarked.

He wasn't as old as I'd first thought, probably in his fifties. He had a shy expression but seemed ready to pass the time of day. I smiled.

'It doesn't look as if you have many volunteers,' I remarked. 'And from what Monsieur Perrault was saying, there's no secretary either. Are you looking for someone? I thought I might apply.'

'The salary's a bit low,' he said. 'Not that it makes much difference these days. We advertised the job and got a hundred replies, and we haven't had time to go through them all.'

'There must have been a lot to do after the break-in,' I said. 'Replacing the computer and everything. Monsieur Perrault told me all about it. Were you here when it happened?'

'No, I was off all week with my back. If I'd been here, it wouldn't have happened. I never leave without checking that the alarm's on and working. But nobody bothered while I was away. You just can't trust people to do things properly. I told them time and time again and no one took any notice.'

His tone of carping grievance reminded me of Ilse Müller. I was about to offer sympathy when the door was flung open and in came Anny Baeke, rather red in the face. Bother.

'Oh, you've finished,' she said. 'Well, the store-room needs tidying up. Down the corridor, next to the office. The key's hanging on the wall next to the desk.'

Monsieur Paul discreetly disappeared. I made my way slowly to the office, detouring through the ladies' room and groaning at the sight of my sweaty, grubby

84

face in the mirror. I smelt of animal waste matter. My feet hurt. I wanted to lie down.

There was no one in the office. It looked like a thousand other small offices, except that the carpet and all the equipment were squeaky-new. The place still smelled faintly of fresh paint. There was a secretary's desk, a metal cupboard against the wall, a couple of chairs with the price labels still dangling from them, and a coffee machine on a table in a corner. A brand-new computer was sitting on the desk, already connected up. The wall calendar was on last month's page. There were no signs of occupation.

I started with the cupboard. It was locked, but I knew from long experience where to find the keys – in the jolly china mug holding pens and pencils on the desk. There was nothing in the cupboard except a pile of colour brochures in various languages describing the work of the shelter. The desk drawers were almost empty except for a few thin hanging files, none of which contained any information prior to the date of the vandalism. Everything seemed innocent in the extreme. The bank statements told me nothing useful, though I noticed that none of the outgoing payments was for more than BF 20,000. There must be another account which took care of the big payments: phones, salaries, taxes, social security and so on. The correspondence was unenlightening, consisting mostly of letters relating to charitable donations. There were the usual utilities contracts and bills, and a file concerning temporary staff. The shelter got all its temps from the same agency in Ottignies. I noted down the name and phone number on a bit of paper and shoved it in my pocket.

The vandals had really done their work well. The only other possible source of information was the computer. I reached for the ON switch.

Footsteps sounded in the corridor. I've always had quick reactions. I shoved the desk drawer shut and leapt over to the coffee machine. As Anny Baeke burst in, still red in the face, I straightened up and said: 'How does this thing work? I could do with a cup.'

'What are you doing here?' she demanded. 'The store-room is next door.'

'Would you like a cup too?' I asked, unwinding the flex and plugging it in. 'Where do you keep the coffee?'

'If you want a drink, there's a vending machine in the entrance hall,' she said. The flush hadn't faded from her face. 'We have no coffee here.'

'I'll go and get one then,' I said mildly. 'Do you want one?'

'No. Take the key.' Anny grabbed it off a wooden board on the wall and held it out to me. She more or less shoved me out of the office and locked the door behind us.

'You can bring me the key when you've finished,' she said, then stood in front of the door as if to protect it, her face a mixture of irritation and alarm.

I made my way to the entrance hall, got my coffee and sipped it reflectively. Why was Anny so agitated? There wasn't anything in the office to get upset about, as far as I could see. Not in the cupboards, anyway. So that left only the computer, didn't it? I'd have to find some way to get a look at that, too.

The store-room was in a mess. There were metal shelves all round the room and up and down the middle, but people had evidently got used to bringing in boxes of stuff and dumping them just inside the door. I'd have to clear the shelves first and then put the new stuff away. I got started with a sigh.

I don't know how long I'd been at it, but I was just thinking about another cup of coffee when the lights suddenly went out. As I straightened up in alarm, the door slammed and I heard, quite distinctly, the key turn in the lock outside, where I'd stupidly left it. I lurched forward in a panic, tripped over something and fell on my hands and knees. My head banged against the upright of the metal shelf, bringing tears to my eyes. Stay put, I told myself. Wait a minute or two.

As my eyes got used to the dark, I saw the faint illuminated rim of the door in the far corner. The corridor lights were still on. Carefully feeling my way, I stumbled across to the door and felt for the light switch. It worked. Relief. I suppose everybody's worst nightmare is being locked up in the dark. Now I was just locked up.

I banged on the door and shouted as loud as I could, but there was no response. It's difficult not to panic in these situations – I could feel the blood pounding in my head. The key had gone, there was light coming through the keyhole. It was nearly six already – for all I knew, the staff would be going home soon. I'd be stuck here all night. Anger and panic rose again and I thumped on the door and yelled with renewed energy – alas, to no effect.

I'd hurt myself if I wasn't careful. Think, Matilda.

One of the shelves was loaded with boxes containing packets of coffee, cans of mineral water and soft drinks, and biscuits. I sat down and picnicked on *eau gazeuse* and *petits beurres* while I reviewed the situation. Edward knew where I'd gone. When I didn't get home, he'd come looking. And even if he couldn't get in tonight, there'd be people around tomorrow. At the worst, I'd have to spend the night here. I wasn't in any real danger.

Or was I? I had no doubts as to who was responsible. It had to be Anny Baeke. The question was, why? What did she have to hide? Suppose she was a dangerous lunatic? Suppose she knew what I was about and was going to come back and finish me off? Maybe I'd find myself on a plane to China to be turned into folk medicine.

I didn't want to spend the night in that room!

87

I was in imminent danger of losing my self-possession. Don't be a wimp, woman, I said to myself. I looked round for a possible weapon and found a paper-knife and a pair of scissors. Not much, but better than nothing. Thus armed, I felt a little less panicky. I settled down by the door with my packet of biscuits, made myself as comfortable as possible and waited. If Anny came back, she'd get what for.

An hour had gone by and I was starting to feel a little cold. I got up and resumed the pounding and yelling, this time using a heavy pencil-holder from the stationery shelf. I didn't feel too guilty about the damage it was doing to the door. When I stopped, there was a silence, except for the hum of the air conditioning. Then I thought I heard a voice. I banged and yelled again. Definitely a voice – no, two voices. Then the sound of running feet in the corridor and someone calling my name. Blessed relief. I hammered some more on the door, shouting. A key turned, the door opened, and I fell out into Jean-Loup's arms. They felt strong and comfortable and reassuring. The brown eyes were startled and concerned. Behind him hovered Monsieur Paul, clutching a large bunch of keys.

'But Matilda, what are you doing here? I saw your car outside and Monsieur Paul said he hadn't seen you leave. I was worried in case there had been an accident.'

I detached myself, somewhat reluctantly, from Jean-Loup's embrace.

'I was locked in,' I said, grimly. 'Someone put the lights out and slammed the door on me. I didn't see who it was.'

'Are you hurt, mademoiselle?' Monsieur Paul asked, his face concerned. 'You look so pale. Shall I get you some coffee?'

'That would be wonderful.' I suddenly needed a cup

88

of coffee more than anything in the universe. Monsieur Paul trotted off down the corridor, shaking his head and tut-tutting to himself.

'What an adventure.' Jean-Loup looked down at me with a rueful smile. 'I'm sorry I wasn't here. How long were you in there?'

'Only a couple of hours, but it seemed like centuries. Has Anny gone?'

'Everyone's gone. Anny must have thought you'd already left.'

I bet.

We walked down the corridor, his arm round me again. My fright and anger were fading. He smelled faintly of some rather pleasant aftershave. In the hall, we all had coffee – I drank mine in one go.

'Are you sure you're all right?' Jean-Loup asked anxiously.

'Fine, now. But I'm starving.'

He laughed. 'Well, I can do something about that. There's a nice little restaurant in Ottignies – we'll have dinner and then I'll drive you home. It's the least I can do.'

'Dinner would be great, but I don't want to leave my car here. Lead the way and I'll follow you.'

I managed a hasty wash, did some repair work on my face and we drove off, leaving Monsieur Paul to lock up. It wasn't far to the restaurant, where a glass of wine restored my equilibrium and a second one helped me to relax. It probably made me relax a little too much, because I found my gaze dwelling on Jean-Loup's dark eighteenth-century face rather too often, and I had to force myself to look down at my plate. That didn't help because his hands were in my field of vision. My thoughts started to wander. He was having a more than slightly disturbing effect on me. And he seemed totally unaware of it.

This wouldn't do. I was supposed to be gleaning

89

information. A lull in the conversation gave me my chance.

'This awful business with Andrieu – what's going to happen to the shelter now?'

'We won't find out till the police discover who killed him,' Jean-Loup replied, with perfect naturalness. 'I saw the lawyers today. Monsieur Andrieu left instructions regarding Les Fauves, but the lawyers won't reveal what they are till the murder enquiry is over. They didn't say as much, but I'm rather afraid that our future doesn't look too good.'

'So the shelter might fold?'

He nodded. 'It's possible.'

'What would you do?'

He shrugged. 'Look for another job.' He saw my expression and laughed. 'Don't worry. It's not the first time. I know the ropes now.'

I took a sip of wine. 'What about Andrieu's other companies?' I asked.

'I didn't know he had any.' Jean-Loup looked surprised. 'But I'd imagine the situation would be the same. The lawyers did say one interesting thing, though. It seems that Andrieu's personal fortune isn't as large as everyone thought. In fact, there's almost nothing. But I don't suppose it matters much, since he hasn't any close relatives.'

I thought about that while the waiters brought the pâtisserie trolley. When we were alone again, I said: 'The police talked to us for ages. Did they interview you as well?'

'I think they've spoken to everyone. I couldn't tell them anything much. Luckily I was having dinner with friends in Lille when Andrieu was killed and I stayed the night.'

He was in the clear then. Warm with relief, I let the conversation go where it wanted after that. When the meal finished, I found myself hoping he'd suggest

90

a drink at his place, but he didn't, and I couldn't suggest one at mine, what with the house full of unwelcome ears and eyes. So we drove decorously back to Brussels in convoy, said 'Goodnight' equally decorously, and separated. It definitely wasn't my night.

Edward appeared while I was getting myself a nightcap and listened to the tale of my adventure.

'You think Anny Baeke locked you in? It could just as well have been the Wolfman. It's a bit of a coincidence that he came back when he did.'

I hadn't thought of that and the idea wasn't particularly welcome. I considered it. 'Why should he?' I asked.

'Why should she?'

'Because she saw me chatting up the concierge and then found me in the office. She's been looking at me suspiciously ever since we met.'

'Well, they could be in it together,' Edward pointed out. 'What are you going to do now?'

'Call Jean-Loup in the morning and offer my services as a secretary. He said at dinner that they needed somebody to do the filing and generally clear up the backlog. It shouldn't be too difficult to persuade him.'

'Under the spell, is he?' Edward enquired. 'You're a chip off the old block all right.'

'Don't let my mother hear you say that. Anyway, you can't talk. Ilse Müller can't see past you.'

For some reason, he looked discomfited, presumably at the mention of Ilse Müller, so, changing the subject, I asked: 'Any luck with PA Express?'

'Not much. They offer a standard courier service – next-day delivery in a variety of countries. They're sending me an information package.'

'Here?' I asked in alarm. 'You didn't give your own name, did you?'

He looked at me with indignation. 'Certainly not. I gave Byron's.'

I went to bed.

Chapter 13

Wednesday started well, with two uniformed cops knocking at my front door and informing me that Inspector Guillaume wanted to see Edward and me in his office. Immediately.

'In my dressing-gown?' I asked indignantly.

'We'll wait,' they said.

While dressing, I took the opportunity to call Richard Grandville on the upstairs extension. There was no fuss or bother. He said he'd meet us at the police station and proved to be a man of his word. I was beginning to think he was worth every penny of the huge fee we'd undoubtedly have to pay him. Guillaume wasn't looking at all pleased. He didn't waste any time.

'I have information that it was you who broke into Monsieur Andrieu's car,' he said to Edward.

How had he found that out? We were up the creek without a paddle right enough this time. I felt like a school-kid caught cribbing under the desk. Edward was quite still. I admired his self-control. My hands were sweating.

'Information from whom?' Richard Grandville enquired mildly.

'Monique Ryckmans,' said Guillaume.

'Was she a witness?' Grandville asked, still in that deceptively mild tone.

'No. She informed me that Monsieur Andrieu knew Dr Haycastle had committed the theft.'

'How?' Grandville asked.

Guillaume's face became an even darker red, and he shifted angrily and impatiently in his chair. 'She wasn't able to say,' he admitted grudgingly.

Sudden realization struck. He was bluffing. He didn't have any proof. Relief swamped me. Behind, Richard Grandville said: 'That's not good enough, Inspector, and you know it. Madame Ryckmans could have all kinds of reasons for implicating Dr Haycastle.'

'I know your clients are withholding information,' Guillaume snapped. 'Andrieu was killed by a .38 calibre bullet. His own gun, which disappeared so mysteriously from that car, used the same type of bullet. We suspect a connection.'

'Have you found the gun?' Grandville asked.

'Not yet. But we will. And if your clients were at all connected with that theft, they'd better watch their backs.'

'You've only got Andrieu's word for it that the gun was stolen in the first place,' I said. 'Suppose it wasn't?'

'Why should he report that a gun had been stolen if it hadn't?' Guillaume asked, blankly.

To take a shot at us, I could have said, but it wouldn't have been wise.

There was a moment's silence, then Guillaume continued: 'Miss Müller has told us that Dr Haycastle threatened to kill Andrieu on Saturday morning. You were there too, I believe, Miss Haycastle?'

'He was angry,' I said. 'He didn't mean it.'

' "You do that and I'll kill you",' Guillaume quoted. 'Those were the words?'

I thought fast. 'English overstatement,' I said. 'We do it all the time.'

'Well!' said Edward, in a pained tone of voice, picking up the cue like a professional. 'The bounder wanted to censor my paper. I could have wrung his neck.' And he looked at Guillaume in well-simulated haughty indignation.

93

I knew exactly what Guillaume was thinking: he thought Edward was guilty as hell but he couldn't prove it – and he was damning all English people to the fiery pits.

'If there's nothing else, Inspector,' Richard Grandville said, rising and zipping up his briefcase, 'I have things to do and so, I'm sure, do my clients.'

Guillaume couldn't stop us leaving, but it had been a narrow squeak. Outside, Edward said: 'What was the point of all that? He knew he didn't have enough to pin us down.'

'He was hoping you'd break down and confess,' Grandville replied. 'Fortunately he underestimated your nerve. Both of you. But it was a close thing. Tell me, how could Andrieu have known about the break-in?'

'He was in the conference room. He must have seen Edward leave and put two and two together.'

'Are you sure nobody else saw you?'

'Positive,' I said. 'The lift was blocked and I'm certain no one followed me down the stairs. Anyway, if someone else had seen us, they'd surely have told the police by now.'

'I suppose so,' said Richard Grandville. 'Incidentally, I have some more details for you about the murder. Andrieu was found dead in his car in the underground car park at the Burgundia Conference Centre, at seven o'clock on Sunday morning, by two of the hotel workers. He'd been killed by a single shot at about eleven o'clock the previous night and from the results of forensic tests, he was killed right there in the car. As usual, nobody heard a thing. No fingerprints, no weapon.'

'Was he in the front seat?' I asked abruptly.

'The driving seat.'

'And the bullet wound?'

'In the chest. From close range, according to the

94

reports. There seems to have been a struggle.'

'And the police think he might have been shot with his own gun?' Edward was thinking out loud. 'Well, that would tie in with our reading of it. He still had the gun in his possession. He and his attacker must have struggled for it and he ended up taking a bullet himself.'

'It's an interesting theory,' said Richard Grandville. 'Except that nobody can prove it was Andrieu's own gun till the police find it.'

He obviously wasn't the kind of man who got excited easily. 'I have to say,' he went on, searching in his pocket for his car keys, 'I think you're both rather lucky not to be in jail. I'd advise you to get on with your investigations as quickly as possible, Miss Haycastle.'

It was good advice.

The next step was to ring up Jean-Loup, which was quickly done. He was only too pleased to have a bit of free help in the office for a day or two, which would give me a chance to get my hands on the computer. That afternoon, while Edward was watching a French film on the telly, I called up the temp agency in Ottignies and asked for the name and number of the girl who had filled in when the mysterious Madame Greenberg resigned. I explained that I was taking over the job and needed to talk to her about a few details and, as I expected, the agency didn't raise any objections. The secretarial world, too, has its good ol' girls' network. Another phone call later, I found myself talking to one Corinne Armand, who was more than happy to take a break from her tedious job to have a nice little chat with me.

'There's nothing to worry about,' she said reassuringly, 'it's a small office and there's not a lot going on. It's just the usual routine – nothing difficult. Correspondence, answering the phone, you know. But watch out for that Anny Baeke – she's a real nit-picker.

Doesn't like anyone muscling in on her territory. She's the reason I left, really. I couldn't put up with it any more.'

'Did Madame Greenberg leave any instructions – about the system and so on?' I asked. 'It's just that I'm having to start from scratch, because of the break-in, and they want me to do it all the same way as before.'

She'd heard about the break-in from the agency. She'd left just before it happened and, as far as she knew, they hadn't taken on another temp after that. Anny Baeke had probably put her foot down. Oh yes, the system. Well, she'd just used Madame Greenberg's files. No, there was nothing unusual about them. Except . . . 'Security,' she said. 'They're nuts about security. Half the documents in the system were protected and I wasn't given the passwords so I couldn't open them.'

'Did they ask you to protect any documents?'

'No. It was all boring routine stuff – didn't need it. Monsieur Andrieu always worked on the confidential files himself. You can ask him if you're stuck.'

'He's dead,' I said. There was a squawk at the other end, followed by a flood of interested questions. I answered as best I could and got her back on the subject, with some delay.

'You don't know where Madame Greenberg went?'

'No, there was no forwarding address. Some private letters arrived for her after she left, but not even Monsieur Andrieu knew where to send them. She's vanished.'

'Well,' I said, 'I suppose it doesn't matter really. All the documents were on the hard disk and that was destroyed by the vandals, so I can't use them anyway.'

'You can always try the back-ups,' Corinne said cheerfully. 'But without the passwords, you won't get much joy out of them.'

Back-ups?

'What back-ups?' I snapped.

'Madame Greenberg was an absolute fanatic about back-ups. Everything was on diskettes. A whole box of them. I saw them myself.'

'Where are they?' I asked excitedly.

'Well, that's a good question,' Corinne answered, a hint of ruefulness in her voice. 'You see, they had the offices redecorated while I was there, and all the furniture and carpets had to be moved out, so I had to pack up all the contents of the cupboards. That's when I saw the diskettes. But after we moved back in, a whole load of stuff had got lost. It wasn't surprising really, because the whole place was in total chaos – you know what it's like when you've got painters in. But Anny Baeke said it was my fault. There was a row and I told her what I thought and walked out.'

'But do you think the diskettes are still there?' I asked. 'And if so, where?'

'They could be anywhere,' Corinne said frankly. 'There were boxes and files all over the place and heaven knows where they all ended up. I didn't have time to ask anyone. But perhaps they're in the archives. You could ask Monsieur Paul. If anyone knows, it'll be him.'

I thanked her and put the phone down, excited. Maybe we were getting somewhere at last.

Edward appeared, looking faintly puzzled. 'Odd film,' he commented. 'I couldn't quite suspend my disbelief. If you'd just been told by your doctor that you had to take things easy and avoid all excitement on pain of instant death, would *you* go and marry Brigitte Bardot?'

Chapter 14

The morning mail brought two interesting missives. There was a packet of information from PA Express addressed to Byron T., which I left to Edward to sort out. The second was addressed to me and contained a single printed sheet. It said, in French: 'Stay away from Les Fauves or you'll regret it.'

'Hello,' I said. 'Take a look at this. No, don't touch it. Fingerprints.'

Edward looked the letter over, and made a clucking noise.

'You'd better not go to Ottignies alone. Tell you what, I'll come with you.'

'Don't be ridiculous, I don't need a chaperon.' Handling with care, I put letter and envelope into a plastic file and gave it to Edward.

'If I'm not back on time, give this to Richard Grandville,' I said. 'But I'll bet you a hundred francs Anny Baeke sent it.'

'But why?'

'That's what I'm going to find out.' I swallowed the last of my coffee.

Byron T. thudded gaily down the stairs and entered the kitchen, his face unclouded. I envied him his carefree existence.

The traffic was bad going out of town, but I got to the office on time, if only just. Not that it mattered, but I like to be professional. Monsieur Paul was his usual friendly self, but Anny Baeke hardly bothered to hide her scowl when she saw me.

'I don't know why Jean-Loup asked you to come – there's hardly anything for you to do,' she said crossly. 'Just a few letters and a bit of filing. I told him I could have done it perfectly well myself.'

'Is Jean-Loup here?' I asked, and for some reason she flushed.

'He's coming in later. I said I'd show you the ropes.'

'Surely you must have more important things to do,' I said diplomatically, hoping she wasn't going to hang around and cramp my style. 'I'll sort myself out, don't worry.'

'Well, I'd better tell you how to work the computer. You might not be familiar with the system. The last girl wasn't.'

I was perfectly familiar with the system. It was the same as I had at home. But Anny didn't seem prepared to leave. She explained the system at length, then hung about, looking over my shoulder, as I started to type the first letter. Page one of the Good Secretaries' Guide: how to get rid of persistent encumbrances. I stopped working, turned right round in my revolving chair, leaned back and smiled up at her.

'It's quite all right, really,' I said amiably. 'If I need any help, I can always come and ask you.'

She didn't like that but it left her with no real alternative. Reluctantly, she backed away and edged out of the room. I breathed a sigh of relief, swung round and got down to work.

There were half a dozen letters written out in Jean-Loup's clear black handwriting, plus a list of phone calls to make, accepting invitations, making appointments and so on. I polished off the lot in less than an hour, did the scanty filing, and settled down to explore the computer. To my utmost disappointment, there was nothing on the hard disk at all except a file of business

99

correspondence, rather badly typed, probably by Anny Baeke herself. I repressed my frustration and thought hard for a minute or two. The phone had a list of internal numbers taped to it. Remembering what Corinne Armand had said, I dialled Monsieur Paul and asked where the archives were. He said he'd show me and five minutes later he appeared, a large key in his hand. Solemnly, we trooped down to the bowels of the building.

Since the building was relatively new, the bowels weren't in too bad a state. Threading his way past old pots of paint, coils of cable and rolled-up ends of carpet, Monsieur Paul stopped in front of a cupboard door marked 'Archives', laboriously inserted the key and opened the door. A mass of squashed-up documents and deformed files met our eyes. There was a smell of very old paper.

'Ah, *ça alors*,' said Monsieur Paul, wrinkling his nose. 'But what are you looking for, mademoiselle?'

'Miss Baeke said some papers had got lost when the repainting was done. I thought they might have got in here. I suppose there's nowhere else they could have gone?'

I was treated to the Belgian shrug, an all-purpose national gesture which conveys ignorance, helplessness, apathy, passivity, disavowal of responsibility, and stoicism in the face of unrelenting fate. I got the message.

I thanked him and promised to return the key when I'd finished. It was a lengthy and completely fruitless search. There was nothing of interest there at all and no sign of any diskettes. I returned to the office, feeling depressed and not quite knowing what to do next. Even I flinched from the thought of searching the entire shelter from top to bottom. And even if we did find evidence of wrong-doing, I thought glumly, that didn't necessarily prove Edward innocent of murder. It only made his story a little bit more plausible.

As the morning stretched on, I realized that Anny had been right. There wasn't enough to do. However, the computer had the usual set of games on it, so I sat and de-mined the oceans until lunch, answering the odd phone call. I ate my sandwich and apple sitting in the shelter grounds and returned, dispirited, to my prison. The afternoon yawned before me, endless. It was a lovely day outside, just the kind of day for a long walk in the forest. The shelter appeared to be deserted. The building echoed with quietness. Jean-Loup rang to say he was running late and would be in later that afternoon. I sat and cracked my jaws yawning.

When Anny Baeke suddenly popped her head round the door, I was almost glad to see her.

'Are you busy?' she asked. 'We need some help with the feeding. Would you mind?'

I didn't mind at all.

I got to do the birds. Quarantine fees are low at Brussels Airport, which makes the wild bird trade particularly interesting to the criminal-minded. Crates of exotic birds arrive every week in ghastly conditions, transported by the most respectable airlines, in total defiance of international conventions. Thousands of them die en route. It makes you want to weep. The shelter had special aviaries for the few that had been salvaged by the overworked authorities. They seemed quite happy flitting round their cages, chirping happily at the sight of the full feeders, but they didn't have a lot to be happy about. Still, at least they were alive.

As I was shaking the bird-seed out of my clothes, Anny came in and said: 'Would you mind just giving these to Lucy?' She thrust a bunch of bananas into my hands and pointed to a door. 'In there,' she said, and disappeared again. Yas'm!

I went in. It was a small room containing a spacious cage, inside which was sitting a large, belligerent-looking chimpanzee. A sign on the cage said, inappropriately, to my mind: 'Lucy'.

I've always differed from most of mankind in that I utterly fail to find chimpanzees cute and amusing. I think it's because their behaviour's too human, which is, of course, why most people like them. Whatever the reason, I always feel uneasy seeing them in anthropomorphic ads for tea and so on, dressed up in silly clothes and doing silly things. Not that Lucy was ever likely to be a TV star. She was a fully-grown, solid, unprepossessing animal, and as I came into the room, she turned her head and bared her teeth at me in an expression that was definitely not a smile.

I approached her slowly, wondering if I ought to introduce myself. Keeping a wary eye on her, I crouched, stretched out my arm and inserted the bananas carefully through the bars of the cage. My luck wasn't in. The bananas stuck briefly, and as I tried to dislodge them, a hairy muscular arm shot out between the bars, grabbed the front of my blouse, and yanked. I might have broken my nose if I hadn't managed to get my hands up to cushion the blow. I found myself chest-to-chest with Lucy, staring into her small, hostile eyes, only the bars between us. Her big yellow teeth were inches from my face. She smelt terrible. I was off-balance, powerless, jammed against the bars.

I have to say quite candidly that I've never been so terrified in all my life. The grip on my blouse was inexorable. I tried to get into a more comfortable position, and Lucy said something in chimpanzee that was unmistakably a threat. She had halitosis.

Without knowing what I was doing, I began to mutter to her. 'Nice Lucy, there's a nice Lucy, good girl . . .' Keep your voice calm and low, Matilda. I hoped I sounded reassuring. I hoped I was talking the right language. For all I knew, she might only understand French. My neck was aching like crazy. My knees were killing me. The bananas lay, uselessly, on the floor of the cage.

Lucy looked at me thoughtfully, reached up her other hand and took a firm grip of my hair. The hand on my blouse relaxed. With a comfortable grunt, Lucy shifted it to my head and started to groom my hair with her fingers. I tried to pull my head away and it was immediately and painfully jerked back against the bars. I wasn't going anywhere till Lucy said I could.

Great. I should have paid attention to that letter this morning. Hell, maybe Lucy had sent it. Should I try yelling? Did I really want to be found in such an ignominious position? Oh God, why do these things happen to me?

My dilemma was solved after ten agonizing, humiliating minutes. I heard Jean-Loup's voice outside, then the door opened and there he stood in the doorway, shocked into stillness. Lucy made a noise which sounded astonishingly like a welcome, and gripped my hair so tightly I nearly shouted. Through my watering eyes, I could see Anny Baeke in the corridor, her hands to her mouth.

Jean-Loup was miraculous. He walked in quietly, crouched down by the cage and talked to Lucy in a voice that would have wrung tears from a Gorgon. He wheedled and flattered and cozened and enchanted her. He was wonderful. He was irresistible.

She watched him, entranced, and I felt her fingers slackening in my hair.

'Don't move till she lets go,' he said to me without changing his tone, and then the sweet persuasions flowed on without a break. A nerve-racking minute later, to my abject relief, Lucy let go of my hair and loped eagerly over to him. I crawled away from the cage, and collapsed in a heap with my back to the wall.

'Dear me, you do seem to be accident-prone,' said

Anny Baeke, her voice fat with satisfaction. I didn't have to look at her to know there was a smile on her face.

Jean-Loup was still sweet-talking that damned chimp, but at that he looked round and said: 'Where's the notice? The warning notice? Matilda should never have been allowed in here.' He sounded angry.

'Someone must have taken it,' said Anny. The satisfaction was suddenly gone; she was looking at him anxiously now. 'I didn't know. It wasn't my fault.'

'You should have warned her,' he said. Getting up, he came over and knelt beside me.

'Warned me of what?' I asked, croaking slightly.

'Lucy has a habit of grabbing people. It's not her fault. She was badly abused before she came to us and she has a lot of behaviour problems.'

A chimp with behaviour problems. I swallowed a pithy comment and massaged my ill-treated scalp.

'You'd better come to the first-aid room,' Anny suggested, moving towards me, the anxious look still on her face. Involuntarily I flinched away, and Jean-Loup said: 'You've done enough. I'll take her there myself.'

The expression on Anny's face would have been sweet revenge for me, had I been in any state to register it properly. Jean-Loup helped me up and supported me down the corridor to the first-aid room. It was hardly worthy of the name, a mere concession to Belgian labour laws. It contained a sink, a camp-bed with no blankets on it, and a large cupboard with a red cross on the front. In the mirror over the sink, I saw my face hatched with red marks where the bars of the cage had been. The skin was broken in a few places. My hair was standing on end. If we'd been in a beauty contest, Lucy would have won.

I was a casualty now and Jean-Loup had no hesitations about touching me. He got cotton-wool and disinfectant and treated my scratches, enquired about tetanus immunity, and then cleaned up my hands, which were also damaged.

'I'll get you a cup of hot tea,' he said. 'Best thing for shock. Lie down and rest for a few minutes. I'll be right back.'

My hair was still on end. My handbag was in the office. Maybe there was a comb in the medical cupboard. I went over and opened the door.

There were four shelves in the cupboard, only one of which was occupied by medical supplies. The top two contained the necessary materials for binding documents: boxes of plastic covers and blue spiral bits. The bottom shelf contained two large box-files clearly labelled on the back: Anita Greenberg.

I was on my knees in a microsecond, my alarms and injuries instantly forgotten. The first file contained papers and an address book. There wasn't time to go through them.

The second file contained six diskettes, neatly bound together with red rubber bands. Bingo! Jubilation. Now, how to get them out of here?

It wasn't difficult. When Jean-Loup came back with the tea, I told him I felt like lying down for a while until I was well enough to go home, and would he be kind enough to bring me my handbag and briefcase. That done, once I was alone it was a simple matter for me to transfer the contents of the files to the said receptacles.

I waited half an hour, then emerged and made my excuses. Jean-Loup offered to drive me home in my own car, and this time I let him. My hands were still shaking, though whether it was my experience with Lucy or sheer excitement at my discovery, I couldn't tell. I sat in the car clutching the bags to my bosom like a miser with his life savings. Jean-Loup saw me inside, exchanged a few words with Edward while we waited for a taxi, and went off with promises to phone and see how I was tomorrow. Neither of us mentioned volunteering for any more work, but he invited me for supper at his flat the following evening. Edward's expression became rather old-fashioned, but I didn't say no. At least something was going right.

Chapter 15

My uncle's reaction to the tale of my misfortune was a hoot of laughter and a flood of monkey stories. After a while, I began to think I'd got off lightly. Monkeys were obviously bad news. With some trouble, I diverted the flow of happy reminiscences and unpacked my briefcase. We were alone in the house; Byron T. was out seeing the iguanodons in the Natural History Museum. In case you should consider this eccentric, I should point out that Brussels has the best collection of iguanodons in the world – around thirty glorious specimens discovered down a coal-mine in the nineteenth century. The palaeontologists weren't sure how to put the bones together at first, but they seem to have got it right now, at least as far as we know.

Together, Edward and I read through the Greenberg papers. I have to say that there wasn't a lot which could be considered helpful. Most of it consisted of photocopies of various official regulations concerning the export, transport and import of endangered fauna and flora, and annexes listing endangered species, potentially endangered species, and species requiring particular vigilance.

'All easily obtainable stuff,' Edward commented, leafing through it. He held out a couple of sheets to me. 'What's this?'

'Extracts from the *Moniteur Belge*.' I took the documents. 'Details on company registration – Andrieu's companies. This'll save me a trip downtown.'

There were four Andrieu companies: Les Fauves, the Burgundia Centre, PA Express and something called PA Entrepôts. Les Fauves, which was listed as a charitable association, had three directors: Philippe Andrieu, Monique Ryckmans and Jean-Loup Perrault. The other three companies were *sociétés anonymes*, or limited companies. In each case, Philippe Andrieu's name was first in the list of directors, and Monique Ryckmans's was second. The other names were unfamiliar.

'What does *entrepôts* mean?' asked Edward, frowning. 'Stores, or something like that?'

'Warehouses. And look at the address.'

'Zaventem Airport,' he said. 'So?'

'So we have an international courier company and warehouses, both located at the airport, and an animal shelter. Where's that documentation you got from PA Express? What are their destinations?'

According to the glossy and impressive brochures, PA Express specialized in serving Africa and Asia.

'He'd need contacts in the main cities,' I said slowly. 'Maybe branch offices. A whole network of collectors. Try this for size. The stuff gets sent here by air, courtesy of PA Express. The live merchandise goes to Les Fauves, the skins and bones and ivory get stashed away in the warehouses till they can be re-routed.'

'Don't the customs do checks?' Edward demanded. 'And what about the TRAFFIC people? Somebody must be in the know.'

'You can buy a lot of silence in Belgium,' I said. 'We're only speculating, remember. But I'd love to see what's inside those warehouses. And I'd give my front teeth for a look at PA Express's files.'

'We couldn't do that!' Edward was horrified. 'Far too dangerous.'

'We couldn't,' I said. 'But Guillaume could.'

'No,' Edward said flatly.

Stubborn old goat.

'You've got to come clean some time, Edward.' I sounded like a schoolmarm even to me. 'Anyway, we haven't got enough to bring Guillaume in. But at least we can pass this on to Richard Grandville. See what he advises.'

'All right,' Edward agreed grudgingly. He hesitated a moment, then said: 'I'm not prying, but have you thought about the Wolfman? He might be implicated too.'

'I've told you, he's in the clear. His story checks out all down the line. I don't suppose he's got the faintest idea what's going on. He's the original innocent. And he adores the animals. You should have seen him with that ape.'

'Hmmm,' said Edward.

'Anny Baeke's a much more likely candidate if you ask me. And I'd dearly love to know why Anita Greenberg left. Maybe Richard Grandville can track her down.'

'How much is he going to cost us?' Edward said, on an afterthought.

I had to smile. 'I'm glad you said *us*.'

'Oh,' said Edward. 'Like that, is it? Enough said. Well, what about these diskettes?'

Edward didn't know a thing about computers. He sat and watched fascinated as I switched on, inserted a diskette and tried to open the first document. Zilch. Same with the second. And so on. Everything, as Corinne Armand had said, was password-protected.

'Well, can't you find out what the password is?' asked Edward impatiently.

'I haven't got a decryption programme,' I said. Edward looked blank. 'You can get specialized software to crack the password problem, but I don't have it,' I explained. 'I could beg, borrow or steal, but it would take a while.'

109

'But in films people are always breaking into each other's systems,' Edward objected.

'Artistic licence.'

'Well, what are we going to do?'

'Think,' I said repressively. 'Most people use pathetically simple passwords – their own names, their wives' names, kids, girlfriends. We'll try a few.'

I tried the names of everybody connected with Philippe Andrieu whom I knew about, including Lucy, and drew a blank. I tried Anita Greenberg and Corinne Armand. Nothing. I tried the company names and initials. I tried the names of all the African countries I could think of. I tried all the Dukes of Burgundy, though even I felt it was a long shot.

'You mean,' Edward said thoughtfully, 'that it could be any word in the world? In any language?'

'As long as it's short enough. It could even be random letters.'

'Anything at all? Countries, cities, flowers, birds, animals?'

'Yes.' There was a short silence. I looked at my uncle. I suddenly felt the hair rising on the back of my neck.

'Edward,' I said. My voice sounded queer. 'Those papers you stole from Andrieu's car. Where are they?'

'I hid them in the garden,' he replied, surprised. 'In your compost heap. Why?'

'Impala, oryx, bongo, okapi. Names of antelopes.'

'Oh no,' Edward said. 'Surely not. That's the wildest hunch I've ever heard.'

'It's not a hunch,' I told him. 'It's a logical deduction.'

It took ten minutes to retrieve the papers from their odorous hide-out. Edward had intelligently wrapped them up in a plastic bag before burying them in the compost, so there was only a slight hint of ripeness about them.

I stared at the piece of paper that had puzzled me when I'd first seen it.

110

'You can't possibly think those are the passwords!' Edward exclaimed. 'Come on, Matilda, you're grasping at straws.'

But they were! They were. Edward and I sat at that machine opening document after document, and although some of them were quite innocuous, others most definitely were not. To start with, there was a whole series of letters to government officials in various countries concerning import and export licences for animals, plants and goods which Edward knew to be on the restricted lists. There were names and addresses in Kinshasa, Nairobi, Mombasa, Bangkok and Delhi.

'These people must all be on the payroll,' I said. 'Andrieu applied for licences in the normal way, and these people granted them in return for a share of the profit. How could they do that? I thought there were controls.'

'In the Third World?' Edward said derisively. 'You get someone to swear that the specimen was obtained legally, that export won't be a problem for the survival of the species, or you say it's for scientific usage or some such thing. Or you just bribe the next man up. There are requests for fairly ordinary species too. Maybe those were used as covers. It's not uncommon to find these goons disguising animals and birds as less rare species to get them in and out. Birds with borrowed plumage and animals with painted fur.'

'And the contacts over here provide the import licences,' I went on. 'Door-to-door delivery. Dead simple. A bit of bribery at the airports and everybody keeps their eyes closed.'

Ivory, tortoiseshell, crocodile skins, little rare monkeys and birds from Africa. Wild orchids and cacti for unscrupulous lovers of exotic plants. Tiger bones, rhino horn and the gall-bladders of bears to keep old men happy in China. It was a profitable little business.

111

'Have you noticed the name of the signatory here?' Edward said, pointing at the screen. I looked. Monique Ryckmans.

'Good,' I said. 'Stuck-up bitch. She treats poor Ilse like dirt.'

The doorbell rang violently, announcing the return of Byron T. Kaplan. He'd had a good afternoon with the iguanodons. I heard him telling Edward all about it, in a flood of schoolboyish enthusiasm, while I prepared supper. He went off to bed early, tired out, no doubt, by his exertions, and Edward and I returned to the computer screen. It was a hard, slow slog, and Edward gave up around eleven. I stuck at it.

The last diskette was the most interesting of the lot. It contained electronic mail files. All the stuff was from the same source, presumably Les Fauves, to three separate e-mail addresses. Andrieu had been using the Internet to communicate directly computer to computer. The trouble was, it was all gibberish, lines of meaningless letters broken up into short groups like words. I couldn't make head nor tail of it. I was getting tired and frustrated so I decided to leave it till the next day.

I took the stuff to bed with me and locked my door, just in case.

Chapter 16

Next morning, I saw Byron T. off to the Congo Museum, complete with written instructions.

'I'm sorry I can't go with you, but we've got some important work to do. Sure you'll be OK?'

'No problem,' he said beaming. 'I wonder, Matilda, when I get back – I've made some notes for my paper, and I'd be honoured if you'd let me show them to you. Will you?'

'I'm out to dinner tonight, but maybe this afternoon?'

'Sure,' he said. 'That'd be fine.'

I wished him a nice day and he set off up the road towards the bus stop.

Then Edward and I returned, as the French say, to our muttons.

Edward was just as puzzled as I'd been by the e-mail files.

'It's all set out like bona fide memos,' I said. 'The *From* and *To* and *Date* are in clear, but the rest is all scrambled. It's got to be a code of some kind.'

'Any common groups of letters?' Edward asked. 'Anything that could be "the", "and", or even "a"? Print out half a dozen and we'll look at them.'

My uncle and I are both crossword experts, but an hour's study of the print-outs was completely unrevealing. We tried out various theories: substituting the previous letter of the alphabet, the next letter of the alphabet and so on right down the line. That took more time and got nowhere.

'What other kinds of code are there?' I asked in despair.

'Thousands,' said Edward unhelpfully. 'One-word keys, lines of verse or songs, popular sayings, combinations of letters and numbers.'

I screwed up my eyes and stared at the printed sheets. Each memo followed the same format. *Date*: day/month/year in numbers. *From*: always the same e-mail address. *To*: three different e-mail addresses, all in Belgium. Under that was typed a one-, two- or three-digit number, and then came the message.

'What do you think the number means?' I asked.

'Reference numbers?' Edward suggested, frowning.

'Are they in sequence?'

'Random.' I riffled through the pages. 'No, these two are the same. Different dates, though.'

Edward took the two sheets and studied them through his bifocals. Then he brought them closer to his face.

'Look,' he said, 'look at this. There are common groups of words. Here, and here. And here too. I'd say the same code was used for both these letters.'

'Do you think they've got a whole series of codes and the number tells them which one to use? But this number's 216. They can't possibly have that many.'

'Yes, they can.' Triumphantly, Edward whipped off his specs. 'In a book, you can have as many pages as you like. It's a book code.'

'How does it work?'

'Easy. Sender and receiver have the same book – same edition too, or it's useless. You pick any page and take a group of letters. Then you equate those to the letters of the alphabet and Bob, as they say, is your uncle. All we need is the book.'

A good night's sleep had restored my scattered wits.

'*Vol de Nuit*!' I exclaimed, and Edward said almost simultaneously: 'Well, I'll be blowed! We must have pinched all his cipher equipment in one go. It was worth the trouble after all. Now let's see if it works.'

It worked. Edward and I scribbled away, our tongues sticking out with concentration, stopping only for minimal refuelling. By mid-afternoon we'd decoded a score of memos. They were all from Andrieu to his local businesses: the Burgundia, the warehouse and PA Express. They contained explicit instructions concerning shipments of goods in and out of the country, with dates, flight times and details. It was a goldmine.

One was particularly interesting. Addressed to Monique Ryckmans at the Burgundia, and dated three weeks prior to the vandalism at the animal shelter, it said simply that the preparations for data transfer to the Burgundia Centre were to begin next day and *the security operation would take place as planned* (my italics).

For some reason, Andrieu had decided that the shelter wasn't safe any more. All the computer data had been transferred down the line to the Burgundia and a few days later vandals wiped the computer clean. A nice touch, since no questions could now be asked by tax people or other interested authorities. Andrieu had hired Jean-Loup and everything was set to go on as if nothing had happened. None of the stuff I was reading would have survived, if it hadn't been for a conscientious secretary.

'Well,' I said finally, sitting back, 'we've got more than enough here to start a full-scale enquiry. This all goes to Richard Grandville in the morning. He'll tell us what to do with it.'

'I could do with some supper,' Edward said, getting up and yawning.

'I bought a couple of vegetarian pizzas.' I folded all the papers up and put them away. 'For you and Byron, if he comes back hungry. I've got a date with Jean-Loup. Dinner at his place.'

Edward turned towards me, suddenly serious. 'Matilda, I didn't want to mention it, but I'm not at all happy about your involvement with Perrault. I know you think he's got nothing to do with it, but if you don't mind my saying so, you may not be entirely unbiased.'

'I haven't got an involvement with him,' I said. 'We're only having dinner.'

'Well, I think it's very unwise.' Edward looked unusually upset.

I sighed. 'Don't worry, he's OK. My nose tells me so.'

'Your nose?' said my uncle. 'I thought it was another part of your anatomy you were thinking with.'

I was starting to get irritated. 'Edward,' I said. 'Don't interfere. It's none of your business.'

'I'm your uncle,' Edward said with asperity. 'That makes it my business. And I don't trust handsome young men with sharp white teeth.'

'I *want* to go, and I'm going. For God's sake, Edward, I don't need a nursemaid. I never did. And I don't need advice on my choice of men, either.'

That escalated the conflict.

'Oh you don't, eh? You haven't exactly had conspicuous success so far.'

'You're such an expert at stable relationships?' I snapped.

We might have started throwing furniture, but the doorbell rang before things got really serious. I let Byron T. in. Edward had stomped upstairs in a rage. I was feeling pretty cross myself. What if I did fancy Jean-Loup? Fancying people isn't a crime.

My face must have shown something, because Byron T. suddenly cut off his flood of happy chatter and asked: 'Say, Matilda, is anything the matter?'

'No, not really. Edward and I had a fight.'

'Nothing serious, I hope?'

116

'No. I'm sure it'll blow over. He thinks I'm still fifteen years old.'

'It's natural he should feel concerned,' Byron T. said diplomatically. 'Being your uncle and all.' He paused, then went on: 'I know you've been trying not to involve me, but Dr Haycastle's in some kind of trouble, isn't he? To do with this murder?'

The blue eyes were looking straight at me. I thought of George Washington. I wished I could tell lies convincingly.

'Yes,' I said, 'he is. Big trouble. We've tried to keep you out of the mess as much as possible.'

'But maybe I could help. I'd be willing to do anything, really I would. Just tell me how. Or even if you only want to talk. I feel kind of helpless just standing by.'

'I really appreciate it, Byron.' I smiled up at the All-American Boy. 'If there's anything at all you can do, I'll ask. Now what about those notes of yours? I've got half an hour before I have to get ready.'

Byron T.'s notes were prolific and disorganized, and turned out to be a panegyric about the inevitable Henry M. Stanley. I gave some cautious advice about the plan of the paper, tentatively suggesting that one or two other explorers might have been involved in the opening up of the Dark Continent. The names of Burton, Speke and Baker seemed to have fallen lightly upon the all-American ears. But in spite of all that, he was a nice boy.

It took much longer than expected, so I had to rush to get ready. Even so, I was nearly fifteen minutes late by the time I rolled up to Jean-Loup's apartment. He didn't seem to mind. He kissed my cheek, took the bottle of wine I'd brought, hung up my jacket and poured me a glass of champagne. He was wearing a loose white shirt and light slacks, and looked like something out of *Les Liaisons Dangereuses*. I was glad I hadn't listened to Edward.

It was a lovely apartment of the sort you can't find

117

in Paris – new, secluded, spacious, balconied, tastefully furnished, surrounded by greenery. Jean-Loup had set the table on the wide terrace and we ate out there with the scent of hot foliage coming up to us and the sound of soft music wafting out. He had the Frenchman's instinctive passion for good food and wine. The troubles of the day receded perceptibly. We talked about Paris; gradually I felt nostalgia and alcohol overcoming any disturbance about my uncle's odd behaviour.

As the evening air grew sharper, we moved inside and Jean-Loup went to make coffee. I wandered round the big living room with its open fire, shining parquet and acres of window, then came back to the deep leather couch and sank into it. It was pristine. So was the expensive, luxurious carpet. All the furniture was brand-new. Jean-Loup came back in with coffee things and a percolator on a tray, which he put down on the rectangular smoked-glass coffee-table. He sat on the couch next to me, his knee almost touching mine, and poured the coffee. Then he stopped and looked at me.

There are moments when you think: 'Here we go! Hooray!' Jean-Loup slid his arm along the back of the sofa and moved towards me. I closed my eyes, in best Hollywood manner, and waited.

The phone rang.

Sometimes I'd like to take every telephone in the world and sink them in the ocean. I sat up. Jean-Loup reached for the phone, said '*hâllo*' a couple of times, stared at the receiver for a moment and then put it down, looking puzzled. He was scarcely back in his place when the damn thing rang again. He snatched the receiver up, spoke more sharply than before, then looked at me and said: '*Personne.*'

'Heavy breathing?' I asked, sitting up once more.

'Just silence. But there was someone there.' He replaced the phone and sat staring at it, frowning.

'Does it happen often?'

'This is the first time.'

The phone rang again and he picked it up, this time with more irritation. Idly, I went to the balcony and looked out and down. It was perfectly quiet, apart from the odd car passing along the wide road beyond the trees. There was nobody in the forecourt of the apartment block. But somebody was obviously out to spoil my evening. If I let them, that is.

'Unplug it,' I said, moving back inside. Jean-Loup looked at me questioningly, the phone still in his hand. I followed the cable to the wall-socket and pulled the plug out. We stood looking at one another, smiling.

I was very glad I hadn't listened to Edward.

It's so nice just to lie in bed with someone, at peace with the world, talking and drowsing and laughing. There was something touchingly naive about Jean-Loup. He was really a child of nature inside a sophisticated body and his simplicity was as refreshing as April rain. All the same, I wanted to get home before daylight, so I dragged myself out of bed, despite his sleepy protests, and went to the kitchen to put on more coffee. It was very quiet outside. I browsed dreamily along the rows of polished bookshelves, listening with half an ear to the gurgling of the coffee machine.

And suddenly dreaminess and contentment vanished like a cat up a chimney. Saint Exupéry's *Vol de Nuit*! The Folio edition. I pulled the book out and stared at it, my heart thumping, conscious of a ghastly feeling that perhaps I'd leaped before looking yet again. Surely Jean-Loup couldn't be ... After all, it was one of the most popular books in the French language – millions of people had it on their shelves. It couldn't mean anything.

His voice called: '*Mathilde!*' from the bedroom, and I jumped and dropped the damned book on the floor. I was picking it up when he appeared, having pulled on

119

his trousers and thrown his shirt on open. His hair was all over his face. I shoved the book back into place and said: 'The coffee's nearly ready.' My voice sounded peculiar to me, but he didn't seem to notice.

He tried laughingly to dissuade me from going, then when that failed, offered to see me to my car. We drank the coffee and went down, his arm round my shoulder.

Most of the lights in the apartments were out, but a couple of fancy lamp-posts were shining in the fore-court. There was just enough light to see by. Enough to see that somebody had spray-painted 'Vache' in red on the bonnet of my car.

We stared with our mouths open. Unlike some capital cities, Brussels is not the sort of town where you expect to find graffiti on your car.

It was a bad end to what had promised to be a perfect evening. The paint was dry already and there was nothing we could do. So we kissed and said 'Goodnight' and I drove home through the empty streets, thinking very hard indeed.

At home, everybody had gone to bed. Even Hortense was nose-down somewhere piling up the zeds. I saw the documents and diskettes stacked neatly next to the computer. They'd be going to Grandville's office tomorrow. Better make copies.

Pushing thoughts of Jean-Loup out of my mind, I sat down and laboriously removed the passwords from all the documents on all the diskettes. Then I copied the files on to diskettes of my own, just in case. It was early morning when I finished and I was cream-crackered. Putting the documents and original diskettes into my briefcase, I took the copies upstairs with me and fell into bed.

Chapter 17

I didn't get an early start on Saturday morning and trailed downstairs in a somewhat crumpled condition to find Byron T. watching TV. In his case, that consisted of continual flicking between an American soap-opera of unbelievable tedium, a satellite sports channel and the CNN international news.

'Edward around?' I asked, yawning.

'Gone out,' said Byron T., smiling round at me. 'About a half hour ago. Do you want coffee? I've just made some fresh. I got some crumpets in your supermarket yesterday, too.'

'Gone out where?' I said, waking up rather abruptly.

'Not sure. There was a phone call. A lady.'

'Who?' I snapped.

'She didn't say either. But I took the call and it sounded to me like that Madame Ryckmans from the hotel.'

Almost without thinking, I turned to the table where I'd left the briefcase. Nothing. The whole damn lot had disappeared.

I think I howled. I may have clutched at my hair. Hortense shot under the table and Byron T. looked at me with his mouth open, half getting up out of his chair. No, *my* chair, dammit.

'Did he take that case with him?' I demanded.

Byron T. thought about it. 'Yes, I believe he did.' He winced at my next few words. Then another horrible thought struck. My car! I scrambled to the kitchen and found my keys missing from their usual place.

'Uh – he borrowed your car,' Byron T. said, peering through the doorway.

He was going to the Burgundia, wasn't he? To talk to Monique Ryckmans, wasn't he? The idiot. The half-witted, moronic, fat-headed nincompoop. What could he hope to achieve, I asked myself, struggling into my clothes. Was he intending a nice little spot of black-mail? Or did he think she was going to confess? She'd probably bop him on the head and shred all the evidence. Suppose, just suppose, I thought, that she'd murdered Andrieu? She'd hardly boggle at doing away with Edward too. And then I found myself rooted to the spot with sudden horror at the thought of yet another possible permutation. What if Edward and Monique Ryckmans were in cahoots? What else hadn't he told me?

'Is there anything I can do?' Byron T. offered, from the kitchen.

'Yes,' I said rapidly. 'I think Edward's gone to the Burgundia. I'm going after him. Will you stay here in case anybody calls, and take messages?'

'Sure, I'll do that. But wouldn't you like me to go with you?'

'No, it's OK, thanks. But you could get me another cup of coffee.'

Working fast, I shoved all the copy diskettes into an envelope, and wrote a semi-legible explanatory note to Richard Grandville. I grabbed the phone and called a taxi, made up, combed my hair, put my shoes on and charged downstairs just as the taxi arrived at the door.

The avenue de Tervueren was almost on our way, so the taxi waited while I leapt out and shoved the diskettes into Grandville's letter-box. He mightn't find them till Monday morning, but at least they were safe. Now for the Burgundia.

The taxi-driver, a young Italian, entered into the

spirit of things and hurled his elderly saloon through the city streets as if battling to snatch the Formula 1 Championship in front of his home crowd, a widespread national fantasy which makes driving in Italy a real challenge. We screeched into the Burgundia forecourt in a cloud of dust. I paid him double and suggested he'd missed his vocation, which made his day. I found my car outside the hotel, graffito and all, but apparently unscathed.

The reception area was almost empty. I didn't stop. I knew exactly where to find Monique Ryckmans. I'd have staked my life that she'd have moved into Andrieu's office by now. Right again. A new shiny name plaque ornamented the door. Not bothering to knock, I just barged in, and I don't know which of the two was more surprised to see me. They were standing each side of the big mahogany desk. She had her yellow suit on. She was leaning forward, her long-nailed hands firmly planted on the desk, as if she'd just delivered an ultimatum. She looked sleek, well-fed and dangerous.

Her surprise at seeing me was intense, but momentary, and I'll swear her next emotion was pleasure. She straightened up, slowly.

'Miss Haycastle,' she said, smiling, 'how nice of you to come. Now it's one big family party. See what a nice present your uncle has brought me.'

The contents of the briefcase were on the desk between them. Edward was staring at me in disbelief. He was white. He said my name falteringly, but I interrupted without ceremony.

'What the hell are you doing? That's our evidence you're giving her.'

'That *was* your evidence,' Monique said, still smiling. Taking her time, she sat down in her big executive chair, and leaned back. 'Not any more. Dr Haycastle has decided not to take any further action in the matter. Haven't you, Dr Haycastle?'

He couldn't meet my eyes. He turned his head away

and looked at the ground, an old, defeated man. I heard him mutter: 'Yes. That's right.'

'So when I have these documents and diskettes destroyed, there won't be anything further to say, will there?' Two victims before lunch: Monique was having a good day. But she wasn't going to have the last word.

'Oh yes, there will,' I said. 'I delivered copies of those diskettes to my lawyer this morning. He'll know exactly what to do with the contents. You'll be under investigation before the end of the day if I have anything to do with it. I've had enough of whatever game you're all playing.'

The smile faded from her face and was slowly replaced by a calculating and thoroughly unpleasant expression.

'What a pity,' she said. 'I can't allow that, I'm afraid. So I'll just have to let you in on our little secret. Dr Haycastle's and mine, I mean.'

'No, you can't,' Edward burst out, turning to her. 'I beg you – don't.' Then, turning to me, desperately: 'Matilda, let it all drop. Please, let it drop. For your own sake. Come away, now, please.'

'What secret? That you and she are in on something I know nothing about?' I said. 'I can handle that. I expect the police can, too.'

Monique burst out laughing, showing all her clean white teeth.

'You see, Dr Haycastle, she hasn't the slightest suspicion. You have been clever, all these years. She doesn't know what I'm talking about, does she?'

Edward slumped down into a chair as if all the strength had gone out of his legs. I glared at Monique, my temper rising at a rate of knots. I don't like being played with.

'What are you talking about?' I said between my teeth.

'I'm quite amazed you never realized before,' she

124

answered, her voice quite clear and precise, like little taps on a xylophone. 'After all, people must have been remarking on the resemblance between the two of you for years. Your mother must have been quite astonishingly clever too, to keep it a secret all this time. There's a good reason for the resemblance, my dear. Dr Haycastle isn't your uncle at all. He's your father.'

Sometimes when you're dealt a crushing blow, your system goes into self-defence and instantly gets the shields up, deferring the mental and physical pain until another time. So I stood there quite steadily in the doorway, knowing that I'd been KO'd but feeling absolutely nothing, while the xylophone went on plinking: 'Most humiliating for your so-called father – discovering that his wife and brother have been carrying on this ridiculous charade right under his nose for so long. And when he finds out you're not his daughter – well, it might even be damaging to his health. He's well over seventy, I understand. And of course there's the public scandal – the English gutter press love this kind of thing, don't they? There's his academic reputation to think of. And your mother's position would be most unenviable too. Such a respectable family. So why don't you just call your lawyer and have him send me the copies, and I'll say nothing more. That was our arrangement, wasn't it, Dr Haycastle?'

The voice went on talking for a while, but it had faded out of my consciousness altogether. I was re-running the Edward tapes in my mind and it all fitted. There was no doubt we were alike – the physical similarity between us had been the subject of comment for so long that it no longer had any significance for me. Our minds worked alike. And it would explain many things that had puzzled me about my mother's attitude to Edward – even her phone call when he first descended on me.

125

I had to get confirmation on this. In what sounded to me like a perfectly normal voice, I said to Edward: 'May I have my keys, please?' I waited while he scrabbled in his pocket, balanced somehow on my feet as if nothing had happened, and took the keys from him. His hand was trembling. Then I turned and walked out the door. Behind me, I heard Edward call: 'Matilda!' and there was despair in his voice, but it had no power to stop me. I walked straight to the foyer, turned into a phone booth, and called my mother in England.

I waited a long time for her to answer, and when she did, I could hear the hum of female voices in the background and the clatter of cups and saucers. An academic coffee-morning, no doubt. Then my mother's cool voice came on, repeating the phone number in her careful way. 'Is Edward my father?' I said, and listened to the crackling on the wire. She didn't reply for a long time, and then she asked, with real terror in her voice: 'What has happened?'

'Is he my father? *Tell me*, damn you.'

I heard her breath catch painfully and wondered briefly, in another emotional sphere, what the ladies of the college were making of all this.

My mother had never lacked courage. She got hold of herself and I heard her say: 'Yes,' with only a slight shake in her voice. Then as she started to say my name, I slammed the phone down, went straight out, got into the car, started up and drove away. After a while I saw a lay-by, so I pulled in and stopped the car. I sat there for a long time, my hands on the wheel as if I were driving. I wasn't exactly thinking. I was in suspended animation. The fact hung in front of me like an arc-light, illuminating and changing years of familiar events and faces, and I sat there and watched the show, emotionless. After a while a police car drove up and parked behind me. A large gendarme got out, came over and asked if everything was all right. I said I'd just had

126

some bad news. He made sympathetic noises, checked my papers, walked round the car a couple of times and said hadn't I better be getting home? The big red face looked as if it would like to offer help but didn't quite know how. As I drove away, I saw him in the rear-view mirror, cap pushed back, looking perplexedly after me. It was past lunchtime already, but I wasn't feeling hungry.

Driving was something to do, so I drove. After a while, I found myself by the Lac de Genval. I parked and walked round the lake mechanically a couple of times, but it didn't help. I must have been looking rather queer, because I caught a few furtive glances from passers-by. I wasn't thinking about anything in particular, and certainly not about what had just happened; my mind slid away from it every time I made a mental approach. At the end of my second tour of the lake, I stopped. I couldn't go round and round like a clockwork mouse all day.

Driving back to Brussels, I hit the Saturday afternoon shopping traffic. I wasn't heading anywhere specific, but eventually I found myself in the avenue de la Toison d'Or and there before me was the tall thin rectangle of the Hilton Hotel. I suddenly felt that I needed a drink. I parked, crossed the road, walked in through the glittering foyer to the bar, and climbed up on one of the high stools.

It's an intimate kind of bar, luxurious and rather dimly lit. There was scarcely anyone there, though I could hear a muted chatter and clatter from the café next door, where they were serving afternoon coffee and cakes. I ordered a gin fizz, I don't know why. I used to drink gin fizzes years ago but I never drink them now. I gave up the hard liquor habit when I discovered good wine. But hell, today I felt like a gin fizz.

A silver bowl of nuts stood on the polished counter

127

- I ate the lot, finished the undissolved sugar at the bottom of the glass, and ordered another. The barman served me without comment and refilled the nut bowl. He was short and stocky, with an impassive brown face. Latin American, probably. He looked tough.

They'd lied to me. All my life, two of the three people who'd been closest to me had been lying. Edward was my father. My father's brother had been my mother's lover. My cool, calm, respectable mother, with her inflexible sense of propriety and her insistence on behaving *comme il faut*, had thrown her cap over the windmill for her husband's younger brother. At that point, my mind refused to look at it any more. I put the problem aside and ordered another drink. I was getting selective about the nuts in the bowl; the cashews were the really tempting ones.

My third gin fizz arrived. I saw the barman make a very discreet negative gesture and turning, glimpsed a young man in the doorway looking at me. He was wearing a suit. An assistant manager, I guessed. Many luxury business hotels have a slight problem with ladies of a certain persuasion. But I wasn't dressed like a high-class hooker, or for that matter a low-class one, and it was Saturday, and there weren't too many bored or lonely businessmen about, so they gave me the benefit of the doubt. The young man nodded and disappeared.

By the time I got to the bottom of the third drink, the bar was starting to fill up. The increasing hum of talk was preventing my mind from functioning clearly. I kept looping round and round the sentence about my father's brother and my mother's lover without it making very much sense. A man said something to me. He looked quite nice and respectable, but I stared at him without understanding and after a while he moved away. I ordered another drink. As the barman put it in front of me, he said quietly: 'Do you want to talk about it?'

I said: 'No,' and he left me alone.

How could they? How could they have not told me? How could they have maintained such a veil of respectability and kept up such an appalling deception at the same time? Like an incompetent video-recorder, my mind kept on showing me my mother, her brows drawn slightly together, saying over and over again: 'Why can he not send things that are sensible? Why can he not send things that are sensible?'

Then I thought about my father – the man I'd thought was my father – with his remote smile, his withdrawn air, his long-distance pride in my achievements. He wasn't a man who found it easy to express his feelings, but that didn't mean he hadn't any. They'd made a patsy out of him too.

Quite suddenly, I couldn't stand it any more. I wanted to get out of there. I dragged out a credit card and waved it at the barman. As he dealt with the bill, I had a fleeting doubt as to whether I could get through the door. Where *was* the door? I could hardly scrawl my signature, and I heard the barman say: 'Let me get you a taxi.' I waved him away and slid off the stool. It seemed a long, long way down.

I could still stand. That was something. I located the door and got out through it. Then in the brightly lit foyer, full of well-dressed people enjoying their Saturday night out, the pain suddenly hit me, so hard that I couldn't even yell. I was immobilized by it, dishevelled, distraught and, alas, irremediably drunk.

The lift doors opened with their usual melodious sound and Richard Grandville stepped out, accompanied by two posh ladies and a posh gentleman. He saw me immediately and stopped as if he'd been shot. Then, to his eternal credit, he moved towards me, not away. I lurched forward too, but my feet were still

129

nailed to the ground and I'd probably have fallen flat on my face if he hadn't caught me by the arms.

'Miss Haycastle, what on earth has happened?' he asked. And I blurted out:

'He's my father. My father. Edward's my father,' and burst into hysterical tears.

I don't recall a lot of what happened after that. I remember being sat down in an opulent leather chair with a box of Kleenex and a large glass of ice-cold water. I remember hearing Richard Grandville's voice giving some explanation to his dinner companions, and the story must have been good because they went off like lambs, with soothing murmurs and sympathetic glances in my direction. The young assistant manager was dealt with in a similar fashion.

I was starting to feel hazy by then. I've got a hard head, but peanuts really kill me. Things were coming and going, and the thought of being sick on the Hilton's nice clean floor was too awful for words. Out of the mist, I heard Richard Grandville say: 'Shall I take you home?' and the thought was so unbearable that I lurched upright and tried to shout: 'No!' at the top of my voice.

'All right,' he said equably. 'You'd better come to us. I'll have to call my wife. Just wait here a minute.'

That's when I went off-line.

Chapter 18

I shall spare you a catalogue of my sufferings when I woke up. Anybody who's been on a real blinder will know how I felt. It was the middle of the night and I was in a strange bedroom. Richard Grandville's house. A little lamp was burning on a table by the bed. There was a litre bottle of mineral water and a glass. I had fallen amongst civilized people. I drank half the bottle of water and felt the twenty tons of pressure on my head reduce to seventeen and a half. But at least I didn't have the bed-spins.

I crawled into the en suite bathroom and splashed my face with water, taking care not to look into the mirror in case I broke it. A pair of neatly folded men's pyjamas was laid out on a wicker chair. I was in my underclothes. I got into the pyjamas and crawled back to bed, switching off the night-light with a grunt of relief.

I surfaced again in daylight. The pressure was down to fifteen, and I felt as if my brain were wrapped in kitchen foil. My teeth were wearing fur coats. On the table stood a fresh bottle of water and a napkin-covered plate containing sandwiches. My stomach growled ferociously. I hauled myself cautiously into a sitting position. I felt maybe I could manage a bite or two. Four sandwiches and a half bottle of water later, I thought maybe I could get up, but when I moved, all the furniture in my head slid across the floor and crashed against the wall, so I desisted. It hurt to think about Edward, so I didn't.

That, unfortunately, gave me time to think about my escapade. What a pin-brained idiot! Getting paralytic in a public place and only being saved from the ultimate shame of passing out in the Hilton foyer by the grace of God and Richard Grandville. What must he think? This is it, I told myself, like thousands of repentant drunks before me. Next time there mightn't be a knight-errant nearby.

After a while I began to look around. It was an expensive but glacial room, decorated in shades of blue. Shiny parquet floor with expensive rugs, dark blue dressing table and bed, flowery curtains, correct but cold. I thought about trying to get to the window to look out, but didn't get any further than thinking.

I heard footsteps coming briskly up the stairs. There was a knock on the door. I tried to say: 'Come in,' but found that my voice was a mere croak. My host appeared, carrying a glass of water and a packet of Alka Seltzer. A practical man.

'I shan't ask how you're feeling,' he said. He popped an Alka Seltzer out of its foil bubble and dropped it in the water. I hate Alka Seltzer. I drank it with my face screwed up and said: 'Yuk!'

'The wages of sin,' said Richard Grandville, sitting on the edge of the bed. A fleeting thought about how I must be looking flashed through my brain. I was glad the curtains were still closed. It was the first time I'd seen him out of a suit; he looked more human in an open-necked shirt and casual trousers.

'I rang Edward and told him where you were,' he said without preamble of any sort. 'Your mother had rung up in considerable distress and he was in a state too. I said you needed some time to adjust and you'd be in touch when you were feeling up to it.'

His matter-of-factness brought me face to face with

the thoughts I'd been avoiding for hours. My world, which had ground to a halt the day before, suddenly lurched and started to move on again. I looked up at Richard Grandville and said dully: 'They lied to me. They've been lying to me all my life.'

'I know. And you're going to have to sit down with them and find out why. There may have been all kinds of reasons. Don't judge till you've heard them. They're still the same people, you know. It's only their relationships to you that have changed. By the way, Edward has admitted that this was the cause of the last quarrel with Andrieu. He threatened to tell all if Edward didn't get off his back.'

'And Monique Ryckmans will carry on the good work if we don't suppress the evidence we found. I left some diskettes in your post-box, by the way.' I was still croaking.

'You told me last night,' Richard said with a slight smile. 'I've already looked at them. I think they should go to the police, but Edward says it's your decision. Why are you frowning?'

'I don't remember telling you that.'

'I'm not surprised. You told me a great deal, most of it totally incomprehensible. But don't worry – I'm positively clam-like when it comes to professional secrets.'

'What do you think of the evidence?'

'I think the police could roll the whole thing up, if they move fast. Leave it too long and the crooks will have time to run for cover. But it's up to you to judge the effect on your family if Monique Ryckmans carries out her threat.'

'What would you do?' I asked, unable to think.

'Get that woman under lock and key as soon as possible. Accuse her of attempted blackmail and have the police keep the details quiet. I've a feeling that if you handed Guillaume all this evidence on a plate, he'd be only too pleased to give you a little help with

Madame Ryckmans. Guillaume's not a very prepossessing individual, but he's honest. He's also rather bitter about being passed over for promotion – a positive result or two would do him the world of good professionally. But as I said, it's up to you.'

'There's only one problem with that.' I leaned back, closing my eyes. 'Now we know what that last quarrel was about. Edward was so desperate to stop the secret coming out that he was prepared to give up his life's crusade. Suppose he was also prepared to kill Andrieu? If I give Guillaume the goods, he'll arrest Edward for murder.'

'That may well happen anyway,' Richard Grandville said. 'There's nothing to stop Monique Ryckmans laying information – a quick anonymous phone call and the job's done. But you were convinced Edward was innocent. Has this changed your mind?'

'I don't know,' I said, and it was the truth.

He left me alone after that and I slept for several hours. I woke up feeling much better. I even managed to get vertical and stay there. There was no sign of my clothes, but I had my handbag, and a dressing-gown had been provided: sober, luxurious dark blue towelling with RG embroidered on the breast pocket. It fitted pretty well; Richard Grandville and I were about the same height. Having done what I could about hair and face, which wasn't a lot, I set off to explore.

My room was on the second floor at the back, overlooking a garden big enough to have mature trees in it. Out in the corridor, there was a tempting smell of something cooking, so I headed for that, nose up like a Bisto kid. The whole house was out of a catalogue. I don't know how people keep their houses looking so incredibly tidy and polished. I never can, but that may be something to do with having a cat like a one-woman demolition squad. Anyway, as I keep telling myself, houses are for living in, not looking at.

134

I found the kitchen on the ground floor at the back. It was a dream: sparkling tiled floor, natural wood finish, double-draining sink, machines everywhere, picture window overlooking the garden, all the cupboard doors properly hung and fitting like a glove. I bet the Grandvilles didn't have any drawers that fell off their runners when you pulled them out. I don't suppose their drains ever got blocked up either.

A young woman was standing by the stove, stirring something in a Le Creuset casserole. She glanced up as I came in, replaced the lid with deliberation and turned to look at me full-face.

She was in her late twenties, with a fit, athletic look and short fair hair. The face was pretty, but rather hard. She was wearing expensive sports gear in an attractive shade of powder blue that went well with her tan.

Her first move had not been welcoming, and neither was her expression. I summoned up all my social graces and said:

'Mrs Grandville, I'm Matilda Haycastle. I'm very grateful to you for allowing me to stay here – I hope I'm not in the way.'

'Oh, don't worry about it. My husband's always bringing home stray dogs,' she said. It was an English county accent, hard and clipped.

Stray dogs? Thanks. I swallowed a tart response. 'I suppose he explained the circumstances?'

'He said something about family problems,' said Mrs Grandville. She stared at me unblinkingly and added: 'Do you think getting drunk's a good way to solve them?'

Who did she think she was, the Salvation Army? I had to remind myself that I was in her house. It was fortunate, on the whole, that the door opened at that moment and Richard came in.

'Ah, you two have met,' he said pleasantly. 'Dinner's

135

nearly ready.' He lifted the lid of the casserole and peered inside. A wonderful aroma filled the room.

'*Navarin d'agneau*,' I said, and he looked round, surprised, and laughed.

'Right first time. Are you hungry?'

'Starving.'

'You must have an iron constitution,' he remarked. 'Ready to eat, Sybil? Come and sit down.'

'I've already told you, I'm going out,' she said, rather curtly, I thought. 'You remember. Emily's wretched hen-party.'

'Oh yes, I forgot. Sorry,' he said. 'Give her my best wishes, won't you?'

She nodded, gave me another straight look and went out, leaving an awkward silence behind her. I was the first to break it.

'You cook?' I asked, parking myself in one of the chairs.

'One of my hobbies. Didn't Georges tell you? I won't offer you a glass of wine, but would you like some grape-juice?'

'Lovely. Have you heard from Georges at all?'

'Not a peep. You?'

'No. He's probably bamboozling some rich American widow on the high seas.'

Richard Grandville smiled slightly. He didn't seem to be a man who did anything to excess. But at least he wasn't asking any painful questions, for which I was deeply grateful. I watched him making a salad.

'No vinaigrette?' I asked.

'Olive oil and salt, Italian style,' he said. 'Vinegar kills the taste of the wine. Georges tells me you're something of a wine expert.'

So we chatted about wine and Italy and Georges, and ate the *navarin d'agneau*, which was excellent, as was the *pêche melba* which followed. Grandville had a pleasant, quiet voice and an imperturbable manner, and because he didn't ask any questions, I found myself telling him things about my childhood which I'd never told anyone, not even Georges.

'I was always on my own when I was a kid. I didn't mind. In fact, I rather liked it. I still do. I just took it for granted that parents kept their distance. I thought all parents were like that. We were like polite strangers living in the same house. It wasn't till I went to school that I realized how odd it was. Then I just assumed they'd drifted apart – lots of my friends' parents were divorced or separated, so it didn't seem out of the ordinary.

'I'm not saying they were unkind or anything. I think my father tried to do his best. He was always very proud of my school results and the prizes I won and so on. It was just that wild enthusiasm was never his style. He expected me to do well and I always did and he nodded his head in measured approval and said he'd expected no less. Whereas Edward –'

I stopped dead. I hadn't wanted to get into that. Richard Grandville looked up and said in his quiet voice: 'Edward . . .?'

'Edward took me out and gave me champagne and we waltzed through Trafalgar Square in the middle of the night and nearly got ourselves arrested.'

'It sounds,' remarked Richard Grandville, 'as if Edward was rather fun.'

'He was. He always seemed to be there when I needed cheering up, too.'

'And do you think that was pure coincidence?' said my lawyer.

I'd never thought about it before, but I did now. After a number of years, you forget the sequence of events and emotions and some digging is required before they resurface. But surely that wonderful day when he'd come down to my school had been just after

137

a speech-day which neither of my parents had been able to attend? Nobody of my own had been there to see me pick up a prize I'd worked six months for. And that time in Paris, was it merely a coincidence that he'd been passing through when I was so unhappy, or had he seen the desperate letters I'd written to my unmoved mother, who believed that trials were good for the soul?

'But how could she have done it?' I asked, staring at Richard. 'My mother, I mean. She always made Edward sound like an unreliable erratic overgrown schoolboy. That's how she talked about him, the way women talk about naughty little boys. When all the time they'd been lovers?' A thought followed which I didn't put into words: a love affair would certainly explain her righteous indignation about all the popsies. 'And above all,' I went on, 'how could they have done that to my father? How could they? Right under his nose.'

'Perhaps you should ask Edward.'

'I don't think I could face him just yet,' I said. 'Though I suppose I'll have to some time.'

'Well, if it's any help, you can stay here as long as you like.' Grandville got up to move some crockery to the sink. I looked at his neat, discreetly check-shirted back and was touched.

'That's very kind, but it's over and above the call of duty,' I said. 'I don't want to inconvenience your wife. She didn't seem exactly pleased to have me here. And I already ruined your dinner last night. Your friends can't have been over-impressed to see a drunken mad-woman lurching out of the bar at you.'

'I don't know,' he said, turning. 'It may be just what my image needs. My friends tell me I'm getting rather staid. Take it day by day. By the way, Edward tells me that Jean-Loup Perrault has rung several times and is anxious to speak to you. And I've had your car brought

over – it's in my garage. We can fetch some of your
clothes if you decide to stay. Why don't you sleep on
it?'

It sounded like a good suggestion.

Chapter 19

I slept on it, but that didn't help. I woke up in the early morning, worrying. Somehow things are always more worrying when you're horizontal. I worked myself into a state of anguish and had to get up and walk round till it wore off. It was useless going over and over it in my mind. I had to do something. And never mind the family tangle – there was still a murder to worry about. Monique Ryckmans might blow the gaff at any minute. But if I did go to Guillaume, as Richard Grandville had suggested, how did I know he wouldn't rush straight out and arrest Edward, and then it would all come out anyway? And what was I going to do about Jean-Loup?

A desert island had never looked so attractive.

I heard an alarm clock ring somewhere in the house, and a few moments later a door opened and somebody went quietly down the stairs. I heard the distant clink of crockery. If I went to Guillaume, wouldn't it look as if I were shopping Edward for revenge? Guillaume didn't like me – that I knew for sure. Or maybe he just didn't like anybody.

I heard steps coming back up the stairs, then the sound of a shower running. Monique, I thought, would hold her hand for a day or two at least. She'd have her own arrangements to make; if she tipped off the police about the blackmail, Andrieu's shenanigans would be bound to come out and she'd have to be long gone before that. She looked to me like a woman with a strong nerve. She already knew Edward was in her pocket. She'd wait to see which way I jumped, and buy an air ticket to Rio just in case.

Something at the back of my mind had been puzzling me, which I hadn't had time to think about. Now suddenly it leapt out. How had Monique known about the information I'd found? Somebody at the shelter must have discovered that the files were gone, put two and two together and tipped her off. Anny Baeke? Or could it, could it have been Jean-Loup? How did they tie in with it all? I couldn't believe, didn't want to believe that Jean-Loup was mixed up in it, but was I letting my feelings interfere? And what about that blasted book?

There was no doubt in my mind that Anny had been responsible for both my mishaps at Les Fauves, and I was pretty damn sure she'd been sneaking about with red paint the other night, but I was somewhat perplexed as to her motives. Simple warnings not to poke my nose in? For if she knew the files were in the sickroom, why arrange an accident that might result in my being taken there? I couldn't get my mind round it.

Maybe the whole plot had been dreamed up by Monsieur Paul, who was in reality a sort of Belgian Moriarty?

The stairs creaked again, and after a minute I heard the clunk of a garage-door and the sound of a powerful car engine. The garage-door closed, the car drove away and then there was quiet.

The question was, why had Andrieu been killed? If you looked at the circumstantial evidence, you had to admit that it all pointed alarmingly to Edward: the long-held grudge, the crescendo of quarrels, the theft from the car, the lack of an alibi. He'd deceived me about so many things. That was what was hurting most, I suddenly realized. But deception was a far cry from murder. Did I *really* think he'd killed Andrieu?

No, I didn't. In spite of everything, I didn't believe it. Edward hated killing. He was one of the few people I have ever known who respect all life, animal as much as human. He had never been able to kill a fly – literally. Would he have sunk all his principles for a moment of revenge? I could believe he might have wanted to, but when it came to pulling the trigger, I did not believe he could have done it.

So who else in all this mess wanted Andrieu dead? Not Monique Ryckmans, surely? Her future was too firmly linked to his. But hadn't she hoped to marry Andrieu and been unable to persuade him? What mightn't that predatory woman do, baulked of her prey? Or what if she was getting over-ambitious and wanted him out of the way so she could take over the scam herself?

And what about Ilse Müller? Unlikely, with her all-important job at risk. But maybe she knew more than she was telling about the animal trade. I hadn't even had the time to ask Edward if he'd found out anything more during his lunch with her. Somehow, it had dropped to the bottom of the priority list.

And then there were Jean-Loup and Anny. If they were involved in the plot, together or separately, there was no way of telling what tensions might exist between either one of them and their late unpleasant employer.

Or maybe it was nothing at all to do with any of these people. Was it some falling-out with his unknown colleagues in the animal-trading business, a *règlement de comptes* of the good old-fashioned kind? If that were the case, then I had to get all this information to Guillaume as soon as possible and have him investigate Andrieu's business dealings properly. If only we could prove Edward's alibi. Maybe somebody had seen him on his long walk from the centre of town to my house? And what about the shot that someone had taken at us in the hotel basement?

Suddenly I had an inspiration. Guillaume thought that Andrieu had been shot with his own gun and that Edward had stolen it from the car. But suppose, as I thought, that Andrieu had declared the gun stolen and used it to take that shot at Edward? If that were the case, and if Guillaume were right about it being the murder weapon, *the two bullets would match.* If, on the other hand, forensic tests proved that the bullets came from different guns, we were looking at a different scenario altogether. That threw the field wide open. Either way, it lessened the burden of guilt on Edward. One thing was clear. We had to find the first bullet.

My mind was made up. I leapt out of bed, threw on my clothes, scrabbled in my bag for Guillaume's number and went to find the phone. Sybil Grandville was standing at the foot of the stairs, obviously just about to go out. A Filipino maid was hovering anxiously with a sports bag in her hands.

'Oh hello,' Sybil said, glancing up at me and away again. 'I'm just off. I'll be out all day. Elena will look after you.' She threw a light sweater round her shoulders and knotted it loosely in front.

'May I make a phone call?' I asked. 'I'll pay for it, of course.'

'Elena will show you where.' Sybil took the bag from the maid's hands, opened the door, and went out without another word. Well, good morning to you too.

The maid was smiling rather hesitantly. I smiled back and repeated my request. Elena led me to what I took to be the study: book-lined shelves, old wood desk and leather chairs, frightfully *House and Garden.* There were two framed photos on the desk: a smiling elderly couple, and a smiling family of four. Parents and brother's brood. No Sybil.

I reached for the phone. Guillaume answered on the second ring, with a snap.

'Matilda Haycastle,' I said. 'I've got some useful information for you. Can we meet? Not in your office.'

143

There was a long silence. I knew I was taking a big risk. If Guillaume was the type of cop who wanted quick results and no bother, then I'd get pulled in and grilled. And all the dirt would come out and Richard Grandville would have to earn his money. On the other hand, if Richard was right and Guillaume was an honest man, there might just be a chance to negotiate a way out of the mess.

The phone slipped in my clutch and I realized my hands were damp with sweat.

'Where?' said Guillaume abruptly.

'In the Bois de la Cambre.' Relief made me stammer. 'The landing stage for the ferry. Half an hour.' I nearly added, 'Come alone,' but that seemed over-dramatic.

'*Soit*,' he said, and rang off.

I'd left damp fingerprints on the phone. I looked at my watch – not much time. I hurried back to the bedroom, fixed my face, and found my way down to the big garage. There was room for three cars in there and my little hatchback was looking lonely in a corner. I wondered what the Grandvilles had thought about the inscription on the bonnet. The garage door was locked and I had no key. Cursing, I dashed up to the phone, summoned a taxi, and reached the rendez-vous point five minutes ahead of time.

It was lovely in the park. Sunlight glittered on the surface of the lake. The small island in the middle seemed deserted apart from a fleet of empty rowing-boats and pedalos drawn up on the shore. The ferry was becalmed on the other side. There weren't many people about – dog-walkers and joggers mostly. It was a beautiful fresh day.

I suddenly felt tired out. I found a patch of dry, relatively clean grass, and sat down thankfully. I was abandoning myself to fate. If Guillaume turned up with half the Gendarmerie in tow, there was nothing I could do about it.

144

He turned up alone, walking swiftly across the grass towards me. He'd abandoned his raincoat as a concession to the summer weather, and was wearing a cheap and ill-fitting suit. He had plain-clothes policeman written all over him. He was scowling. I got up, brushing grass off my legs.

'Well?' He stopped in front of me, nose up. I pulled myself together.

'Let's walk,' I said.

We paced solemnly round the lake, in and out of the tree-shadows, and I told him, with some difficulty, the whole story as it now appeared. He listened without interrupting, though he made a noise like a grunt when I told him about Edward breaking into the car, and again when he heard about the blackmail. I made rather a mess of the whole thing – for some reason my brain was functioning as if there were dirt in the fuel-line.

When I'd finished, he said nothing for a long time, while our feet carried us on round the lake and back to where we'd started. I stopped, feeling as if I couldn't go a step further.

'Well,' I said, 'are you going to arrest us?'

He waited a moment, then replied: 'No. I'm going to try and find that bullet.'

I had to sit down again then, and managed to do so without it looking too much like a collapse, which it was. Guillaume stood staring at me for a moment, then, with some hesitation, he folded himself uncomfortably down on the grass beside me.

'I'll need the diskettes and papers,' he said, staring at the lake.

'I'll get them to you. And Edward's alibi?'

'I'll do what I can. We'll try and find out if anyone saw him walking home on the night of the murder. And if the two bullets do match, that lends strength to your theory that the gun was never stolen.'

145

'Have you found the gun yet?'

He shook his head sombrely. I looked at the angular profile, the unhealthy skin, the lank hair cut crookedly at the back of the neck.

'Do you think Edward did it?' I asked.

'I don't think anything. I look for evidence,' he replied in his curt way. His suit smelled of mothballs and cheap deodorant.

'I know you don't like me,' I said doggedly. 'Or Edward either. But everything I've told you is true. Please believe me.'

He stared at me. Then, abruptly: 'What makes you think I don't like you?'

'Everything.'

He looked down at his knees.

'It's not you,' he said suddenly. 'Or your uncle.'

'What then? We've never met before, as far as I know.'

'No.' He resumed his study of his knees.

My tired brain clicked over the possibilities and came up, somehow, with the right combination.

'Luc,' I said. 'Something to do with Luc.'

An early leaf came drifting down from the tree above us, and landed in a leisurely manner on Guillaume's shoulder. He didn't seem to notice.

'Vanderauwera blocked my promotion,' he said. 'He considered me a complete zero. He made sure I got all the unimportant jobs while he had the good ones. He wasn't much liked. And – I'm sorry – there were a lot of unpleasant things said about you at headquarters.'

Learning that people have been bad-mouthing you is tough on anyone's self-esteem. In my current fragile state, I felt ludicrously like howling. Instead, summoning up my Girl Guide training, I quelled my trembling chin and said: 'I see.'

We sat in silence for a minute or two. A football

thudded past us, followed by a small panting boy. He picked the ball up, bounced it once and made a creditable attempt at a goal kick. The ball shot into the lake, to shouts of anguish from the rest of the team.

'Why did you decide to tell me all this?' Guillaume asked suddenly, dragging my errant attention back from the kids. 'Revenge on your uncle?'

'No,' I said. 'I hate mess and this seems to be as messy as things get. Richard Grandville said you were an honest man, so I decided to trust you.'

To my surprise, a red flush came over his face. Blow me, he was blushing. I stared in amazement, which made it worse, of course. To cover his embarrassment, he got clumsily to his feet. I got tiredly to mine and said: 'Thanks for agreeing to meet me. I'll get the stuff to you as soon as I can.'

He muttered something indistinct, turned and strode off towards the road. A toddler on a tricycle cannoned into his legs and went flying, with howls of indignation. He stopped in confusion, picked up toddler in one hand and trike in the other and reunited them. Then he hurried on and got into a battered old car which was parked on the grass. I watched him disappear, wondering if I'd made a terrible mistake.

Chapter 20

The nearest taxi-rank was in the place Marie-José, so I walked there, rather slowly, and was ferried semi-comatose to Richard Grandville's office. He was with a client and I waited, dozing in a comfortable chair, for an hour. When I told him what I'd done, the dust really hit the fan.

'You've done *what*?' he exclaimed, his voice rising in a most unlawyerly way. He got up from his chair, his face a picture of alarm. 'Why on earth didn't you call me first? Don't you realize that you could have incriminated Edward and yourself a hundred times over? How do you know Guillaume wasn't wearing a wire?'

'What?' I bleated.

'They might have recorded your conversation with hidden microphones,' he said, spelling it out. 'It was a foolhardy thing to do. What's the point of having a lawyer if you don't listen to him?'

'I did listen to you,' I protested. 'You said Guillaume was an honest man, and I thought you were right.'

He groaned and sat down again, hands to his head. I stared in amazement. The whole world was going bonkers.

'Listen,' I said. 'It was all right. He understood. He's going to look for the bullet.'

'What bullet?'

'Dr Haycastle's magic bullet,' I said, and began to laugh helplessly.

I think he realized then the state I was in, because he calmed down, fetched a glass of water, lent me his handkerchief and requested a re-run of the whole conversation. I obliged. He made notes. At the end, he said: 'Well, it's done. Maybe it's all for the best. I suppose you want me to take the stuff to the police?'

'Yes, please.' I said gratefully.

'I'll do it this afternoon. But first, lunch. You look as if you could do with something. I've just got to make a few calls.'

I hadn't had any breakfast, which was contributing to my feeling of being on another planet. I made my shaky way out into the reception area and waited. The secretary kept giving me covert glances from behind her big shiny desk. I wondered how much she'd heard. Everything, probably. I thought that I ought to call Jean-Loup. The door opened and Richard came out.

'We're going to lunch, Alice,' he said to the girl. 'I'll be back at three. Please reschedule my two-thirty appointment.'

'*Oui, Maître*,' she said demurely, and I could feel her speculative gaze resting on us all the way out of the door.

Richard's car was just like him: modestly expensive-looking and exceedingly efficient. He drove calmly and competently. We went to a small but very good Italian restaurant and had an excellent meal. I ate like a pig. Life-function readings returned to somewhere around normal. I tried to pay for lunch and was told coldly not to be ridiculous. It annoyed me. I looked at him for a moment and said: 'You've done quite enough for me already, you know. I don't like being under obligations.'

That got under his skin. 'My dear girl,' he said, signing the credit card slip, 'it'll all go on the bill, don't you worry.'

There was a silence. Then, as the waiter took the

little silver tray away, Richard said: 'I apologize. That was churlish of me.'

'I upset you. I'm sorry too. It's been a rather eventful two days.'

'The British understatement.' He began to laugh. 'Georges said you'd be a new experience for me and he was right. By the way, if you are staying on, I could go round to your house this afternoon and bring some things back. Perhaps you'd like to let me know what you need?'

I recognized a tactful way of asking me what my plans were. The trouble was, I didn't have any. But I couldn't very well skulk at Richard's for ever. Either Edward and Byron T. would have to move out of my house, or Edward and I were going to have to make it up.

'You'll have the house to yourself tonight,' Richard added. 'Sybil and I have got a dinner engagement. I hope you don't mind?'

Mind? It was a relief. I postponed the decision till the next day, and gave Richard a short list of things I needed. I was too tired to refuse his offer of a lift home and anyway, I didn't have any keys. I thought I'd better call Les Fauves, but Jean-Loup was out, so I left a message, conscious of creeping relief. My feelings about him were terribly mixed up and I didn't really have a clue what to say to him. Then I collapsed into bed. It was very quiet in the house. I was missing Hortense. There was no pattering of paws, no sploshing and scritching sounds, no urgent demands for food, or love, or lettings in and out. It was uncanny.

I slept for the rest of the afternoon. I didn't hear Sybil come back in. Richard arrived home late and in a hurry, informing me as he rushed upstairs to change that he'd passed all the documents and diskettes to Guillaume. He hadn't had time to go to my house but he'd phoned, and Byron T. would be coming round

150

later with my things. I stayed out of the way till the Grandvilles were safely off to their dinner, then got my own ready: fresh bread, mozzarella cheese and salad.

I hate waiting for people to arrive. I couldn't settle to anything, and found myself pacing up and down and glancing out of the window every two minutes. At ten to nine, the phone rang. I was expecting Byron T., but it was Jean-Loup.

'I got your message,' he said. 'What's happened? There are policemen crawling all over Les Fauves and half my staff's missing and your uncle's being mysterious. Are you all right?'

He sounded genuinely concerned.

'Fine,' I said cautiously. Guillaume obviously hadn't wasted any time. 'It's all rather complicated. I'll explain when I see you.'

'I miss you,' he said, and I'll swear he meant it. 'I need to talk to you. I know it's late, but can we meet tonight?'

'I'm sorry, but tonight's not possible. Can you tell me on the phone?'

'No. I have to see you. Tomorrow morning? Ten o'clock? At my place?'

I agreed and rang off, and immediately started worrying. What could he want to talk about? Could it have anything to do with Andrieu? Or was it something about us? And why couldn't he tell me on the phone? Why on earth had I got myself into this in the first place?

My cogitations were interrupted by Mr America, who turned up bang on the dot of nine, blooming with health and cheerfulness.

'Dr Haycastle told me everything,' he announced, handing over a large carry-all. 'So now I can really be of some help to you.'

'Everything?' I asked, startled. I was beginning to

151

feel that this case was getting ahead of me.

He nodded, brimming over with sympathy. 'He's really upset about what's happened. He wants to make it up to you. Gee, Matilda, there isn't anything he wouldn't do. Even go to the police.'

'He's too late,' I said. 'I've already been. Didn't Richard tell you?'

Byron T.'s eyes grew round. 'You don't say! That sure must have taken grit. I do admire you. I hope you don't mind me saying this, but I never met anyone like you before.'

A double-edged compliment if ever I heard one. He'd be telling me I reminded him of his Mom next. I said something kind and offered him coffee, then regretted it, because he accepted with joyful alacrity. Then I felt guilty; after all, he was only trying to do his best. We sat at the kitchen table for a long time, and Byron T. told me about his boyhood dreams of becoming the most famous zoologist in the world. I watched the open face and round blue eyes, thinking that he probably hadn't changed a jot since those innocent days. It was impossible not to like him.

We were interrupted by the sound of the car coming into the garage, and a moment later Richard and Sybil came up the stairs from the basement. I glanced at my watch – it wasn't particularly late. Richard was looking rather tired, but Sybil appeared to be in a plain bad temper. Scarcely glancing at us, she swept on past and up the stairs without a word.

Taking the hint, Byron T. leapt up and made hasty excuses, and I saw him to the door. On the step, he paused. 'I was nearly forgetting. That German lady called for you. You know, Mr Andrieu's secretary – what's her name?'

'Ilse Müller?'

'That's the one. She'd like you to call her.' Then he said respectfully: 'May I kiss you goodnight, Matilda?'

'Of course,' I said, offering my cheek. Instead I found myself taken firmly into a large and competent pair of hands, and enveloped in one of the most comprehensive clinches it has ever been my privilege to experience. I was too surprised to struggle – thoughts of boy-scout innocence went flying out of the window. After all, since when have boy-scouts been innocent? He broke it off before it became embarrassing, said: 'Goodnight,' and disappeared. There was a certain jauntiness in his walk.

Behind me, Richard Grandville said dryly: 'I didn't realize you knew him that well.'

To tell you the truth, neither did I.

Chapter 21

I found it difficult to sleep that night, though whether because of the kiss or all the other disturbing factors, I couldn't tell. It was becoming monumentally clear that I couldn't put off facing Edward much longer. I wanted to go home. I wanted this whole thing cleared up. To be frank, I wanted to be shot of the lot of them. I'd go and see Edward in the morning, after talking to Jean-Loup.

I was just dozing off when I became aware of voices somewhere in the house. Talking loudly. No, quarrelling. I sat up. The Grandvilles. I recognized Sybil's voice easily – she was making no attempt to keep it down.

'It's no good arguing, Richard. I want that woman out of my house tomorrow. And this is absolutely the last time you bring any of your down-and-outs home. Do you hear me? This isn't a bloody hotel.'

Richard's voice, answering, was too muffled for me to hear, but the reply came through loud and clear.

'I don't care what the bloody circumstances are. I've had enough of it. Either she goes or I do.'

This was followed by the sound of a door slamming violently and determined steps going upstairs, no doubt to the spare room.

There's nothing worse than finding out you're the skeleton at the feast. It's a horrible, humiliating position to be in. It wasn't Richard's fault but I couldn't stay any longer. My resolution reinforced, I managed

154

to get four hours' sleep and got up looking like a bad make-up job for a horror film. Sybil was not in evidence. Richard Grandville eyed me beadily, but said nothing, which must have taken a megalithic amount of self-control. I told him I was going to see Jean-Loup. He made no comment, but something in his face suddenly made me wonder how much else I'd told him that I didn't remember.

'And then I'm going round to see Edward and sort everything out,' I said, cradling my coffee cup in both hands and staring hard into it.

'Would you like me to go with you?' he asked immediately. Then he frowned and said: 'No, damn it, I can't. I have to be at the Palais de Justice all morning. Are you sure that's what you want to do?'

'Yes, I'm sure.' I paused. 'I haven't thanked you properly for everything you've done. I don't quite know how I'd have got through if you hadn't picked up the pieces. I know it hasn't been easy for you. And please don't tell me it'll all go on the bill.'

'It's been a pleasure,' he said, looking as if he really meant it. He went on: 'I'm sure it'll all go well, but just in case anything happens, you can always come back if you need to. I'll give you a spare key to the garage door.'

He couldn't have been more considerate, especially since he and his wife had been fighting like billy-goats over me. Having extracted a promise that I'd call and let him know how it all went, he went off to work. I put my things into the carry-all, made the bed and left the Grandville house with more than a little relief. It was another lovely day, all new and unspoiled.

I got the car out, still bearing its scarlet inscription. Somebody once told me that taking taxis in Brussels works out cheaper than running a car, but there's nothing like independence. I was early and, to my surprise, Jean-Loup was waiting for me outside his apartment block. The sight of him brought a sudden rush of emotion and I hugged him for a long moment. If only I could be sure. Maybe I should just come right out and ask him?

There was a little sheltered garden by the side of the building, with a couple of rustic benches. We sat down, very close together. There followed an unusually awkward silence.

Silences between new lovers are harbingers of doom.

Jean-Loup said: 'I've been offered another job.'

There had been no time to sort out this new relationship, with all its complications. But of every possible outcome, I had never expected this.

'Where?' I asked.

'Rome. You've heard of the Abruzzi National Park? They've been reintroducing wolves into the wild down there, and now the French government wants to set up a research unit to see if we can do the same in France. They want me to head it up. I went for the interview a couple of months ago but nothing seemed likely to materialize for at least a year, so I had to take the Andrieu job instead.'

'And now it's come up?'

'Yes, the government's finally released the funds.'

'I see. When would you go?'

'Well, that's just it,' he said, apologetically. 'It would be as soon as the police clear up Monsieur Andrieu's affairs. They said I could go now, since I'm not personally implicated in the investigations, but the future of the shelter is in serious doubt and I don't want to go till it's sorted out. But this new job is the one I really want.' He paused for a moment and then added: 'It doesn't mean the end, you know. We can write.'

That was it. First the answer to my doubts. Then the kiss of death. Long distance love. Waiting for letters that didn't come and spending exhausting and unsatisfying weekends travelling to snatch a few hours together. No thanks.

'Yes, I expect we could,' I said, crushing my bitter disappointment. There wasn't much else to say so I changed the subject: 'What were the police doing at the shelter yesterday?'

'Looking at everything,' he said simply. 'Do you know what's going on? They seem to suspect some kind of criminal activity. Everybody's been questioned.'

'It looks as if Andrieu was involved in the illegal animal trade,' I said. 'The shelter was probably the headquarters, at least until that break-in. Now all the data's been transferred to the Burgundia. I expect that's crawling with policemen too.'

The dismay on Jean-Loup's face was, thank goodness, unmistakably genuine. I suppose it was a small consolation to know that my instinct about him had been right.

'Do you mean I've been involved without knowing it?' he exclaimed, getting up and staring down at me.

'It looks very much like it. I think quite a few people are in the same position.'

He sat down again, shaking his head.

'I can't believe it. I've devoted my life to protecting animals and Andrieu knew it. How could he do this to me?'

'That is precisely why,' I told him. 'You gave him instant respectability.'

'Oh my God!' He seemed really upset. Naivety is a poor weapon against the dastardly. I was thankful I'd been born with a healthy dose of cynicism. To take his mind off his troubles, and because I wanted to know, I asked: 'Have the police spoken to Anny?'

'No. They wanted to, of course, but she seems to have disappeared. Nobody knows where she is.'

'Anny's disappeared?' I asked, sitting up sharply.

'I haven't seen her since the day before yesterday. Why?'

'Because I think Anny's in it up to her neck. I think she was the one who locked me in the store cupboard,

157

and she certainly engineered my encounter with Lucy the other day.'

He stared at me in amazement. It had obviously never occurred to him. He looked in need of sympathy but, after the morning's revelations, I just didn't have the energy.

'I'm afraid I have to go,' I said. 'An appointment.'

'Can I see you tonight?' Jean-Loup was studying my face anxiously. 'Will you come round?'

'It depends how things go today,' I replied. 'Maybe tomorrow.'

We walked back towards the car in silence, a little uncomfortable. I glanced up at him and was about to say something when there was a sudden flurry of wild movement, a shout from Jean-Loup, and I found myself drenched in something nasty and cold and wet. I'd shut my eyes and put up my arm in automatic self-protection, and my face wasn't touched, but my shirt was soaked and clinging and I could feel the stuff running down inside my skirt-band. I opened my eyes, saw I was covered in blood, and shrieked in horror. Then the smell of the stuff got through to me. Paint! Red paint! I must have looked like Medea after the murders.

Recovering, gasping from the shock, I became aware that Jean-Loup was struggling with a flailing, kicking figure – an all too horribly familiar figure. It was Anny Baeke, her face so distorted with yelling that she was almost unrecognizable. '. . . nothing but a *tramp*! She's only just met you and she's sleeping with you already, and then last night I saw her carrying on with that American boy *as well*. She's taking advantage of you – you don't know what kind of a woman she is! *Une salope!*'

Jean-Loup had her by the wrists and was staring at her bemused, clearly out of his depth. Time for the Florence Nightingale act again. I stepped in and fetched her a sharp slap on the side of the face, and I have to say that, apart from the therapeutic value, I really rather enjoyed it. She stopped yelling instantly and stared as if seeing me for the first time.

'It was you who painted my car?' I said tightly.

She nodded hesitantly.

'And you locked me in the store-room?'

'The store-room?' she repeated, her brow wrinkling.

'The night Matilda got locked in,' Jean-Loup said impatiently. I could see that he didn't like her very much. 'That was you.'

'Oh no.' She looked up at me in bewilderment. 'I never locked you in anywhere. I went home early that evening.'

I shook my head as if to clear it.

'But it was you who deliberately arranged for me to get mauled by Lucy?'

'Yes,' she said, her voice very small. She looked the way little kids do when they drop their ice-lollies on the pavement.

'But *why*?' asked Jean-Loup, staring down at her with utter bewilderment. She looked up at him blindly, the proverbial frog at the feet of the proverbial prince. Her face went all red, her lips began to tremble and she burst into hysterical, blubbery tears.

Nurse Haycastle took over. I carefully explained the nature of sexual jealousy to an embarrassed Jean-Loup. I calmed Anny down, provided her with a hanky, assured her I would only press charges if she did anything else deranged, detailed Jean-Loup to see that she got home safely, and asked him to let me into his flat so I could get myself clean. The Good Luck Fairy hadn't abandoned me entirely that morning: the paint was water-based and came off relatively easily. My shirt was ruined, though. Without compunction, I borrowed one of Jean-Loup's, made myself a cup of coffee and sat down to drink it.

159

Poor Anny. Poor, poor Anny. Sitting out in the dark, alone, unloved and miserable, while Jean-Loup and I were inside in the light and warmth. Weeks spent worshipping his every movement, reading significance into his most casual word, living from day to day in the hope of seeing him, even if only for a few minutes. We've all been through it, usually around the age of sixteen. Like mumps, it's worse the later it comes. And she must have been lurking outside Richard's house the previous night and seen Byron T. kiss me goodnight so uncharacteristically. Poor Anny. And the daftest thing was that she needn't have bothered getting jealous, because he was leaving town anyway.

He was leaving town. Damn, damn, damn.

Then I remembered something else. If Anny hadn't locked me into the store-room, who had?

I suddenly felt that the last thing I needed today was a confrontation with Edward. I'm not Superwoman. It would have to wait.

Where was I going to sleep that night? Chez Grandville was out of the question. So was chez Haycastle. There was only one answer: a hotel. I decided against the Hilton. Halfway to a small discreet hotel in Ixelles, I remembered that Ilse Müller wanted to speak to me, so I changed course and made for her block of flats. I rang and there was no answer. The entrance hall was full of junk mail and looked rather unkempt. The inner door was wedged open with a piece of folded cardboard, so I was able to go right in to Ilse's front door. But my ringing and knocking produced no reply, which seemed odd. She hadn't collected her mail that morning – the letters were still sticking out of her mailbox in the hall. I rang the concierge's bell. After a lengthy interval, a small fat man emerged slowly from the depths and stared at me suspiciously. In answer to my question, he rubbed his chin and said No, Madame Müller hadn't gone out today, not as far as he knew.

Maybe I was upset by the morning's events or maybe it was the old Haycastle nose, but this just didn't sound right. I floated the suggestion that maybe Madame Müller was ill and couldn't come to the door. This elicited a non-committal shrug. Could I go round the side of the building and look in at the windows? If I wanted to; it was none of his business. I hopped over a short box hedge, negotiated a bed of rather daunted roses and peered into Ilse's living-room window. The curtains were drawn nearly together. In between, I could see the electric light shining.

That did it.

I marched back in, dragged the unwilling relative of Cerberus from the depths again and insisted he open the door for me. He argued he couldn't possibly do that without Madame Müller's permission. I told him Madame Müller might be ill and if he didn't help he'd be guilty of non-assistance to an endangered person. I mentioned Inspector Guillaume. At that, Cerberus cracked. He found the key and opened the door and I charged in like the cavalry in a John Ford film.

Lights were on in the kitchen and living room, which were neat and empty. Ilse was lying on her bed in the darkened bedroom, fully clothed, her handbag, spectacles, a glass and an empty pill bottle standing tidily on the bedside table. She was still breathing, but only just. The concierge stood with his mouth open while I called an ambulance, swearing over the slowness of the telephone operator. I'd forgotten the address and had to ask so I could tell the rescue services. I hadn't the faintest idea of what to do in the way of first aid, so I covered Ilse with the eiderdown and sat holding her hand till the ambulance arrived, which it did very quickly. I gave the guys the bottle, which was marked with an unfamiliar medical-sounding name, and they wheeled her out through the small excited crowd that had gathered at the sound of the siren. I followed the ambulance through the streets to the hospital at top speed.

I answered all the receptionist's questions, as far as I could, then sat, all thought suspended, on a cheap plastic chair in a bare waiting room until somebody came out, some time later, and told me Ilse was going to be all right. I heard out a long dissertation about sleeping pills and stomach pumps and critical time periods, and then asked if I could see her. Tomorrow, they said. I ought to go home. Come back tomorrow.

Chapter 22

It was late. I thought I'd better let Guillaume know what had happened, so I searched the hospital corridors for a public phone and called him. He wasn't at his desk, so I left a message. Then I got into the car, feeling a thousand years old, and drove to the hotel. The room was beige and had a bath. I picked up the phone and called Richard.

'Listen,' I said, 'I'm in a hotel.'

'What? What happened? Didn't it go as planned?'

'Not exactly. It's a long story.'

'You should have come back here. You can't stay alone in a hotel.'

'This is nearly the twenty-first century. I'll be OK.' I was amused by his old-fashioned concern. 'Anyway, they say guests and fish start to smell after three days, and I was near my expiry date.'

'Give me the address and phone number.'

I complied.

'What about telling me about it over dinner?' he suggested. 'I'm not busy tonight and Sybil's out with her friends.'

'Fine,' I said.

'I'll pick you up in an hour.'

'Fine,' I said again.

I ran myself a hot bath, using up all the hotel's bath gel, then lay down in it for a long think. Things were starting to take shape in my mind. I'd been trying to find a common cause for everything that had happened, but the evidence wouldn't fit any of the theories we'd come up with. And my brain had been fogged up, first by Jean-Loup and then by Edward's little piece of news. I had to start from the beginning and think it all through again.

The result was, of course, that first my bath got cold and secondly I kept Richard waiting for a quarter of an hour. He didn't seem to mind. We ate in a very pleasant Thai restaurant near the University, and I told him about Ilse. He listened, frowning, then said:

'How did your meeting with Perrault go?'

In the panic about Ilse, I'd almost forgotten about my jolly morning.

'He wanted to tell me he'd been offered a job in Italy. He's leaving as soon as the enquiry's finished. Then Anny Baeke jumped out of the bushes and threw red paint all over me.'

'What?' exclaimed Richard incredulously.

'The incident with the monkey and the graffito on my car – that was Anny. Nothing whatever to do with the murder or anything else. She's nuts about Jean-Loup and madly jealous of me. She's been following me around for the last two or three days, spying.'

'Good God,' he exclaimed. 'Have you reported it to the police?'

'No,' I said. 'Poor Anny's miserable enough already without that. I don't think she'll do it again. Anyway, Jean-Loup's leaving town so she's got no reason to be jealous any more.'

'You should mention it to Guillaume,' Richard advised. 'Just in case anything else happens.' He poured me another glass of mineral water. I was still off the sauce. I might have an iron constitution, but there was no point pushing my luck.

'The funny thing,' I pursued, 'is that the other "accident" – when I was locked in the store-room – wasn't Anny at all. At least, she denied it.'

164

'And you believe her?'

'She had no reason to lie. That means it must have been one of the other shelter employees.'

'Or Perrault,' Richard said.

'No. I trust him.'

'Because you slept with him?'

And as I stared at him incredulously, he looked into his glass and said: 'Sorry, that wasn't very professional, was it? You'll have to forgive me. Your personal life is none of my business. Have some more chicken.'

Women are always being accused of letting their emotions overrule their common sense, but for my money men are just as bad, if not worse. I was getting a little bit pissed off with all this disapproval from my masculine entourage. What had it got to do with anyone but me?

I was about to say so, when something rather desolate in Richard's face stopped me. Forty-eight hours in his house had made me wise. He was unhappy enough without me making things worse. So instead I said: 'Thanks, I will,' although I didn't really want any more, and changed the subject.

After all the traumas of the day, I have to report that I slept like a log that night. Mindful of Richard's advice, I tried to phone Guillaume before checking out of the hotel next morning, and failed. It didn't matter because his long face was the first thing I saw when I walked into the hospital. He looked as if he'd been up all night. I thought something must have happened to Ilse, but he reassured me. He'd just arrived and the doctors had told him she'd be OK. He hadn't been allowed to see her and was on the point of leaving. I told him about Anny and he listened frowning. A frown seemed to be his natural expression. After a moment's silence, he said: 'We found the bullet.'

We found the bullet. Just like that.

'Is it . . .?' I started, and he nodded and said: 'You were right. From the same gun.'

165

'I knew it!' I exclaimed, beaming.

Guillaume was still looking like a particularly wet weekend. 'We can't draw any conclusions till we find the gun,' he reminded me.

'I realize that. How are the investigations going into Andrieu's affairs?'

'Well,' he said. 'Yes, going well. We've impounded all the documentation from his four businesses, and we should be able to make arrests soon.'

'And Monique Ryckmans?'

'Ah yes. Madame Ryckmans is on her way to South America.'

'Rio de Janeiro?' I asked, breathless. He nodded, and looked amazed at my crow of triumph.

'She'll be picked up there,' he said, 'and put on the first plane back. We have a lot to talk to her about. And Mr Andrieu's other employees, too.'

'Jean-Loup Perrault?' I asked.

Guillaume shook his head. 'He's in the clear, but the caretaker has some questions to answer. And your Madame Baeke. We're trying to get hold of this mysterious Madame Greenberg, too.'

'So we've done it? It's a success?' I was searching the unrewarding face for signs of pleasure or, indeed, any human feeling.

'Yes,' he said. 'That is – there's a possibility it might get swept under the carpet if it proves too embarrassing for the government. There are a few highly placed people involved.'

'Tip off the animal organizations, all of them. They're a powerful pressure group. They'll make sure it doesn't get buried.'

He looked at me in surprise, thought about it and nodded slowly. I thought somewhat sourly about the irony of me giving the Belgian police advice. The irony was lost on Guillaume. He got up. 'Let me know if you hear anything else. Do you have any idea why Madame Müller might have wished to commit suicide?'

'No,' I said. 'Apart from the fact that she's over fifty, out of a job, and may have to go back to Germany to look after her aged mother.'

He stalked off down the hall on his long thin legs, resembling nothing so much as a Meccano construction. I pondered anew about frogs and princes.

Guillaume hadn't managed it, but I didn't have any trouble getting in to see Ilse. She was lying back with her eyes closed, as pale as her pillows. She looked younger without her thick glasses. I thought she was asleep at first, but she opened her eyes at the sound of the door closing and peered anxiously at me.

'Hello, Ilse,' I said. 'It's me, Matilda Haycastle. How are you feeling?'

What a stupid question to ask a woman who's just tried to kill herself.

Ilse said, in a husky voice: 'Is that policeman still there?'

'No, he's gone.' I came over and sat in the tubular chair by the bed. Ilse pulled herself upright and groped on the bedside table for her glasses.

'How did you know?' she asked, still in that husky whisper.

'I found you,' I said. 'I got a message that you wanted to talk to me, and I came round to your flat.'

'Oh yes. I had forgotten. I thought – you would not call.'

'What did you want to tell me?' I asked gently.

Her eyes filled with sudden tears. She groped weakly under her pillow for a hanky, took the glasses off with a shaking hand, and mopped her eyes. I got out of the chair and sat on the bed, putting a hand on her thin arm in the horrible hospital nightie. 'Don't cry. Maybe I can help.'

167

'I am so afraid.' The words burst out hoarsely through the hanky she was holding to her face. 'The police came to me and said they had proof that Monsieur Andrieu had been involved in crimes. They searched my flat and took away papers. If they find out what I have done they will put me in prison. I am so afraid.'

I took her firmly by the hands and said: 'Listen, Ilse. Whatever you've done, the best thing is to get it all off your chest. That way at least it won't be hanging over you any more. And maybe it's not as bad as you think.'

'It is,' she moaned, looking at me through her misted lenses. 'It is. I am a criminal.' And then she said, desolately: 'What will Dr Haycastle think of me now? He has been so kind – so kind. Nobody has ever been that kind to me before. I am so alone. So alone.' The tears started to trickle helplessly out from under her glasses again.

Poor Ilse. What a bleak life it must have been. Clearing my throat and resorting to briskness, I said:

'Edward's in a lot of trouble. If you can tell us anything at all about Andrieu, it might be of real help.'

'Would it?' she whispered, mopping her swollen eyes. 'Would it really?'

'It would,' I said firmly.

It was a pathetic story. Ilse had worked as Andrieu's private secretary for years without suspecting a thing. Then three years ago, he'd given her a surprise. He'd used his African connections to organize a holiday for her – a safari in Kenya and Tanzania with all the trimmings. A dream holiday. It had been the best three weeks of her life. On her last day, he'd called her Nairobi hotel and asked if she wouldn't mind bringing him back a package from a business acquaintance. Quicker than the postal service, and it wasn't heavy to

168

carry. He cautioned her jokingly about bringing back any illegal souvenirs in her luggage, which had made her check everything three times over and leave behind a small ivory bangle which she'd bought for her mother.

Ilse called in at the address he'd given her, received the package and caught her flight with no problems. There were none at Zaventem either, and she'd brought the package to Andrieu the next day. He worked from home, and her own desk was in a small cubby-hole in his house, overlooking the garden.

Ever the efficient secretary, the first thing Ilse did was open the mail. Inside the package from Africa was a sealed Jiffy bag. And inside the Jiffy bag were a dozen or so sachets of white powder. Ilse's first thought was why on earth he'd asked her to bring sugar sachets back to Belgium, but then her brain began to work and she realized what they were. We've all seen smuggled heroin on the TV and in films.

Mechanically, with care, she re-sealed the Jiffy bag and put it on Andrieu's desk with his other mail. Her feet carried her back to her desk and she went through her day's work like an automaton, but her universe had slid from under her. Her trusted boss was a criminal. She was a criminal herself, because she'd brought the stuff back. If she reported him to the police she'd be implicated herself. She would lose her job. She would go to prison. Everyone would know – her mother's neighbours in Frankfurt would read about it in the papers. The family would be disgraced.

Ilse decided to say nothing. Andrieu said nothing. Life went on as normal. Until the day before yesterday, when presumably Guillaume's men had turned up and reawakened the nightmare.

By the time she had finished, I was holding her hand. She lay back exhausted, the tears drying on her face.

169

She seemed calmer now. 'What shall I do?' she whispered.

'I'm going to ask my lawyer to come and advise you,' I said firmly. 'Don't worry about the cost – I'll handle that. But listen to what he says and take his advice. I'm sure he'll be able to sort it out. Don't worry about anything.'

'You're so kind,' she said, her voice nearly extinct.

'Tell me something else,' I said. 'Anita Greenberg was mixed up in all this, wasn't she?'

Ilse nodded, closing her eyes.

'She and Mr Andrieu had been – involved – a long time ago. She was ready to do anything for him.'

'So what happened? Why did she leave?'

'He met Monique Ryckmans. You know – you know what Monique is like. She has no mercy. Anita could not bear it any longer. So she left.'

Innocently leaving behind the evidence that would sink them all, I thought grimly to myself. A time-bomb, sitting patiently in the medical cupboard at Les Fauves, waiting to go off.

'Do you know where Anita went?'

'Switzerland. Geneva, I think. But I do not have the address.' The bony hand came out and grasped my sleeve feebly. 'Miss Haycastle, will you – will you do one more thing for me?'

'Of course,' I said.

'Ring – ring Mutti. Ask her to come.'

I found her mother's number in Ilse's handbag and went out to call. I got through straight away and was mildly pleased to discover that my German was still equal to the task. I didn't mention suicide – I just said there had been an accident and Ilse was in hospital, out of danger, and had asked for her. The old lady must have been way over seventy, but she was brisk and matter-of-fact and said she'd come as soon as she could arrange for someone to look after her dog. I told

170

Ilse the good news, then called Richard and let him know that I'd found him a new client.

I replaced the phone on the hook and gazed glumly up and down the hospital corridor. There was nothing else to do here. Now I'd have to do what I'd been trying to put off for days. I had to go and see Edward.

Chapter 23

My street was deserted as I drove up and parked but, as I got out of the car, my front door opened and Yasmina came out. I'd forgotten it was her day – to tell the truth, I'd lost track of time. A grin appeared on her face and she gave me an energetic wave as she crossed the road, silver bracelets jingling and earrings dancing.

'Anyone at home?' I asked, locking the car.

'Edward's there. And that American creep.'

I stared in surprise. 'Why d'you say that? Don't you like Byron?'

'Can't stand him,' said Yasmina buoyantly. 'He tried to chat me up and when I said I wasn't interested, he turned all nasty.'

Behind her and across the road, the front door opened again and I saw Edward standing there. All thoughts of Yasmina's problems went out of my mind.

'Well, I'd better be running,' she said. 'See you next week.' Then she was gone.

I crossed the road.

'Hello,' Edward said. 'I'm glad you came.' He seemed his usual urbane self. I hadn't expected contrition, but I couldn't stop my anger returning. He stood back to hold the door for me and I went in, feeling like a guest in my own house. Everything was sparkling after Yasmina's visit. I went into the living room and Edward followed me. Hortense, sitting on

172

the window-sill, looked at me as if I were a stranger. Byron T. was parked in front of the TV. He zapped it off as I came in and got up.

'Hi, there,' he said. He looked quickly at Edward, then back at me. He didn't exactly shuffle from one foot to the other, but the effect was the same.

'I just want to say this to both of you,' he announced, 'and I hope you don't mind. I'd be real proud to have you as my daughter, Matilda, and I'd be real proud to have Dr Haycastle as my father.'

It wasn't fair of me, but suddenly his homespun wisdom got right up my nose and my temper, regrettably, slipped its leash.

'That's particularly noble of you, Byron,' I said, 'since considering Edward's record and the fact that he knew your mother, it might well turn out that he's your father too.'

Byron T.'s face went the colour of wet cement. Edward frowned consideringly and said: 'No, no, the dates are all wrong,' which was so typical that tension made me give a gasp of laughter, though laughing was the last thing I felt like doing.

'Listen, old chap,' Edward turned persuasively to Byron T., 'Matilda and I have a lot to say each other, and if you don't mind, we'd rather be left on our own.'

As Byron T. made himself scarce, I threw my bag down on the sofa, threw myself down after it, and said: 'OK. I'm listening.'

'I don't quite know where to start,' Edward began.

I wasn't in the mood to help him. I waited. He shoved his hands into his pockets and stood with his back to me, looking out of the front window. Hortense stared up at him, all ears and golden eyes.

'I suppose a little family history is in order,' he said. 'Your parents got married in '56. The same year I first ran across Philippe Andrieu, as it happens. Funny coincidence. Anyway, I didn't get back to England till

173

the summer of '58 and that's when I met Claire for the first time.' He gave a short laugh. 'You didn't have to be particularly gifted in psychology to see that Claire and Malcolm weren't getting on. They were totally unsuited to each other. Malcolm's always been a dry old stick and Claire likes the good life.'

'Why did they get married then?' I asked.

'She married for security.' Edward's voice held a trace of irony. 'They'd had a bad time of it in northern France during the war. Your mother was thirteen when the war ended, and all she wanted was to get out and escape into another world. Malcolm represented solid respectability, and there were all the academic honours too. She told me she'd been dazzled by the prospects.'

'So what was in it for him?' I asked.

'He fell for her,' Edward said simply. 'Your mother was very beautiful in those days, you know. Malcolm didn't know much about women. He was the hiking, mountain-climbing type – shorts and long socks and cold baths. When they fall, they fall hard. But I don't think either of them kept their illusions for long. Anyway, by the time I got home in '58, Claire's illusions were thoroughly gone and Malcolm had retreated into his ivory tower. So she and I were alone together for the whole summer.'

'You fell in love.'

Edward shrugged. 'If you want to call it that. We were both young. Claire was bored stiff. We used to come up to London together and do the theatres and go to parties – I knew lots of people. We had fun. Claire needed that. She was stuck away in some crumbling university town never seeing anyone except half-baked students and elderly dons with one foot in the grave. And Malcolm's always been rather suspicious of fun. Thinks there's something un-English about it.'

'But he was your own brother,' I said helplessly.

There was a moment's silence.

174

'It's a lie, you know,' Edward said abruptly.

'What is?'

'The idea that blood's thicker than water. It's a lie. I grew up with Malcolm and I can't say I was ever close to him. He was middle-aged from birth. Always telling me I couldn't do things. Always cutting his coat according to his cloth. He was never prodigal.'

'And you were?'

'I've always felt that you only get one innings, so you'd better make the most of it. Your mother was deeply unhappy, you know. She was on the edge of a nervous breakdown when I met her. She hated England, she hated the academic life and she was in a fair way to hating Malcolm and everything he stood for.'

'So you stepped in and saved her?' I couldn't keep the irony out of my voice. Edward turned round.

'Look,' he said, 'I'm not making excuses. I'm explaining, as one adult to another. Be honest, Matilda. You know how these attractions happen. It comes out of a clear sky and before you know where you are, it's irresistible. And when the circumstances are right, it's almost inevitable.'

Yes, I knew. My poor mother. How could it have been otherwise? The prodigal brother returns, arms laden with gifts from exotic lands, hair bleached by stronger suns than the south of England's, blue-eyed, laughing. Ninepins would have had nothing on it.

Edward sat down in a chair opposite me and leaned forward, his forearms on his knees, his hands loosely clasped.

'Then we found out you were on the way and things got serious.'

'It was an accident?'

'As far as I was concerned, yes,' he said cheerfully. 'Contraception was a bit iffy in those days. But I've always wondered about Claire – I know she wanted

175

children and she'd just about given up hope of having any with Malcolm. Anyway, it was too late. You were already more than a twinkle in anyone's eye.'

'So you decided not to tell him?' I said.

'Claire decided,' Edward replied. 'I wanted to, but she wouldn't let me. She didn't want Malcolm's career jeopardized by a scandal. You can imagine the headlines – "Leading scientist's wife elopes with brother" – that would have sent a delicious thrill down the backs of the powers-that-be in academe. And she didn't want a divorce either. Malcolm was earning good money and I was penniless apart from the grants. And I had expeditions planned out for the next five years. Claire couldn't see herself living under canvas for the rest of her life, or bringing up a child under those conditions. Anyway, she thinks I'm fundamentally unreliable – she always has.'

'You lied to both him and me. You cheated us.'

'From one point of view, yes. But it seemed the lesser of two evils. Malcolm wanted a child – he was delighted when you were born, though he may not have shown it. And Claire changed the minute she knew she was pregnant. All she thought about was what was best for you. She became a model wife and mother. And she has been ever since.'

'And what about you?'

'I was back in Africa when you were born,' he said, getting up and moving to the window again. 'Claire wanted me to stay away. I tried to, but every now and then, it got too much for me and I had to come and see how you were getting on. Not as often as I'd have liked, but too often for Claire. There was a row about it finally, and she put her foot down. I think Malcolm was rather jealous too – thought I was a bad influence on you and all that.'

He turned and looked earnestly at me. 'Claire made the right decision, you know. I'd have been a lousy

176

father. Claire and I'd have been quarrelling long before you were born if we'd gone off together. Babies, nappies, pushchairs and so on – not my cup of tea at all.'

'So that's why you stayed away?'

He nodded. 'I regret it now, my dear, believe me.'

'So do I,' I said slowly. 'We'll have to do better in the future.'

Since I claim to be a fairly cool sort of person, I'll skip over the next ten minutes or so. After we'd sorted ourselves out and I'd called my mother and had a word or two with her, and we'd had a cup of coffee, I filled Edward in on the past few days' events. They might have lost their importance somewhat compared to our personal upheavals, but there was no getting away from the fact that a murder charge still hung over Edward.

'What I don't understand,' I said finally, 'is how Andrieu and Monique Ryckmans found out about the family skeleton. Who knows about it?'

'Nobody, apart from Claire, you and me. Nobody. I never told a soul.'

'Did you write letters?' I asked.

'Yes. We corresponded regularly until you left school. Claire kept me up to date on your progress. But I always destroyed her letters and I know she did the same with mine.'

I sat down. Unconsciously I lowered my voice.

'We know that bullets from the same gun killed Andrieu and nearly got us. We've assumed that it was Andrieu who shot at us, and that the gun was in the car when he was killed. But there's another interpretation. How about if somebody else took the gun, shot at you and then killed Andrieu?'

'But who on earth would? And why?' Edward demanded, staring.

'I've had a lot of time to think during the last couple of days, and some of it's starting to make sense.

177

Suppose, just suppose, someone knew not only about the family skeleton but about your grudge against Andrieu? Suppose somebody had a grievance against you and wanted to set you up? What better way than to engineer a public quarrel between you and your known enemy, and then make it look as if you'd killed him?'

'Nobody could have planned it,' Edward said abruptly. 'Plans never work out that well.'

'I don't think it was planned,' I said. 'It's had the look of a seat-of-the-pants affair right from the beginning – that's why the police aren't getting anywhere. Try this on for size. Somebody saw you go down to the basement, or saw me, and followed us down there. That somebody nipped in and had a good old rummage round, maybe looking for evidence against you. Instead he found the gun, whipped it and made himself scarce.'

'Or herself,' Edward observed grimly. 'Tell me why?'

'To try and kill you,' I said. 'That note you thought came from Andrieu could have come from anyone. You went down to the basement again and somebody shot at you. Follow me so far?'

'Only you came down and whoever it was missed, then those Papua New Guineans turned up, or whatever they were,' Edward said, musingly.

'So our friend decided to try a new tactic. Information was passed to Andrieu about the skeleton, and Andrieu used it to try and blackmail you. You had a couple of public quarrels, culminating in the unfortunate words "You do that and I'll kill you", and lo and behold, Andrieu is duly bumped off and you look the most likely suspect.'

'We still don't know for sure that Andrieu's gun is the one involved.'

'Occam's razor,' I said.

'And you think the same person's behind it all?'

'I'm sure.'

'Well,' said Edward, thinking. 'The day we were shot at, the only suspects present in the hotel were Ilse Müller and Monique Ryckmans. And the evening Andrieu was killed, everybody had alibis except me.'

'Monique Ryckmans rang you on Saturday morning,' I said. 'What did she say?'

'She blackmailed me to get the diskettes.'

'But how did she find out about them? It wasn't through Jean-Loup or Anny – I've cleared all that up. And it couldn't have been anyone else at Les Fauves. Nobody knew about them or they'd never have been left in an unlocked cupboard. And how did she find out about the skeleton?'

'Andrieu must have told her.'

'But he couldn't have. I think they must have guessed that you were responsible for the car break-in, but Monique can't have known about the skeleton or she'd surely have told the police when she denounced you. At that stage she was trying her hardest to have you put away. No, somebody told her about the diskettes and the skeleton *after the event*, and there's only one person it could have been.'

I watched Edward's mind going through the various possibilities, arriving at the answer and rejecting it.

'*Byron?*' he said incredulously. 'Impossible.'

'No, it isn't. His alibi on the night of the murder is me – and I was out for the count. *I didn't see him between 9 p.m. and breakfast next day.*'

'He was ill in bed the morning we were shot at.'

'We've only got his word for that, and for all that convincing detail about his taxi journey. He could easily have been at the Burgundia hours earlier, either by taxi or more likely by hired car. He must have hired a mobile phone too. That's how he called me at the Burgundia, and probably how he called Monique on Friday.'

'Great Scott,' said Edward. 'But why on earth should

179

he want to kill me? And how could he have found out about the skeleton?'

'From his mother,' I said. 'Professor Jo-Ann Henderson. You were lovers, weren't you? You must have given her a hint, or perhaps she saw one of your letters. We can find out anyway. And as soon as the police get hold of Monique, she'll spill the beans.'

'But she doesn't know who I am,' said a soft voice behind us, and we turned to see Byron T. in the kitchen doorway, leaning nonchalantly against the door-frame. He had a gun in his hand, but it wasn't pointed at us. It was drooping negligently and no doubt deceptively towards the floor. The round, good-natured face wasn't good-natured any more. It looked watchful and rather emotionless.

'It was an anonymous call,' he said. 'I disguised my voice. So it's right back to square one for the police.'

'That's Andrieu's gun,' I said. It was a statement rather than a question.

'Yup. It's the one that killed him. They'll find that out when they find you. I haven't quite figured out what the scenario's going to be. There are two possibilities. You stole the gun and hid it, Dr Haycastle, but your daughter found it and was so mad at you about the skeleton, as you folks call it, that she shot you and then killed herself. Or else you killed her because she'd found out you killed Andrieu and then you shot yourself in remorse. Which version do you prefer?'

'Neither,' Edward said. He was a little tauter in face and voice than normal, but he was acting up well. I hoped my performance was as creditable.

'You arranged the accidents?' Edward went on, moving slightly in his chair. 'In England and here?'

Byron T. smiled. 'Not the one here. I rather fancy that was your friend Andrieu's idea. But the one in England was mine. An amateur's attempt. I'm glad it failed. This all turned out to be more fun.'

'You followed me down to the car park and saw

180

what Edward was doing? And you stole the gun and took a shot at us with it?' I was determined to test my theory if it killed me, which it probably would.

'Yup. I figured I could get Andrieu blamed for that if I succeeded. But I'm not sorry I missed. This way's better. I had no idea about the old beef between you and Andrieu, Doctor, but it was a real godsend. I knew he'd try to shut you down in some way, so I kind of encouraged him. His blackmail made you threaten to kill him, nice and publicly, and then the night you didn't come home, I knew I was in business.'

'Just out of interest,' I said grimly, 'how did you manage it?'

'Easy.' Byron T. was smiling. 'I was just waiting for the opportunity. You said yourself that you were out for the count that night. I'd made sure of that. You got a good night's sleep, didn't you, ma'am?'

'Knock-out drops?' asked Edward incredulously. I was speechless.

'Corny, but effective,' said Byron T. 'I was at the Burgundia by ten-thirty. Andrieu thought I was going to hand over some papers incriminating you, Doctor.'

'But instead you shot him,' Edward said. 'You were bloody lucky nobody heard you.'

'I'd told Andrieu to make sure there was nobody about. I was home by eleven-thirty. Reliable old Avis. The only risk was if you'd got home before me, Doctor. But I took a chance you wouldn't. And even if you had, you'd have found my door locked, as usual, on account of the cat. I'd had my own keys made, you see, ma'am. And my window's easily accessible from the outside.'

'You thought of everything,' I said grimly.

'I think so,' he replied.

'Just tell me one thing,' Edward said. 'Why? Why did you bother? What on earth have you got against me? What have I ever done to you?'

'Nothing,' Byron said. 'Not to me. It was Mom. I

can't let you get away with the way you treated Mom. You cheated her and you ran out on her.'

'Nothing of the sort.' Edward was emphatic. 'We parted the best of friends. We both knew it was only a short-term affair. She had a boyfriend back home. A chap called Elmer Tibbett, I believe.'

Elmer Tibbett? I glanced at Edward, somewhat puzzled. He shifted a little more in his chair, so he was almost facing Byron, free of the table-legs. Free to move. I caught on.

Keep the big palooka talking.

'Byron, you've got the wrong end of the stick,' I said. 'Surely your mother doesn't hold anything against Edward after all these years. It's ancient history.'

Byron's face was remote.

'She cried and cried,' he said, his voice almost murmuring. 'She never got over it. She still talks about it now. It really meant something to her.'

'Rubbish,' Edward protested. 'It was just a flutter, Byron, really. It didn't mean anything much to either of us. It was the sun and the sand and so on, and working so closely together. It wasn't a real love-affair at all.'

Byron T. looked up at that, and red came into his face.

'Jesus F. Christ, I'm not talking about that!' he exclaimed. 'It wasn't the goddamn love-affair. It was the cricket. Haycastle's cricket. That's what I'm talking about, for God sakes.'

'What?' I said feebly.

'She found the cricket. It was *her* goddamn cricket. Only she was stupid enough to tell you about it and she let you send in the papers and claim the discovery as yours. It wasn't Haycastle's cricket at all. It was Henderson's goddamn cricket. She could have been the one that got the applause and the invitations to talk here, there and everywhere. She could have had

182

her name in the reference books. She never forgave herself for letting you get away with it. She could have been famous and so could I, and you took it all away from us.'

He looked like a red-faced little boy, but the gun was pointing at us now. I looked at Edward: 'Is it true?'

He didn't answer for a moment, then slowly he nodded. 'I'm afraid so,' he said. 'She did find it. She didn't realize it was a new species, but she found it. She brought it to me and I saw what it was and I didn't say anything. It was the only time I'd ever discovered anything new and I didn't want to share it. So I didn't tell her. I just went ahead and claimed it as mine.' He looked up at Byron T. and said: 'I was wrong and selfish to do that, I admit it. If your mother wants, I'll put it right. I'll correct it. There's no need for this.'

'You think you can put it right?' Byron T. asked softly. 'After thirty years?'

I realized I was about to shuffle off this mortal coil for the sake of an insignificant bug I'd never even seen. My mind was a total blank. I'd been through too many emotional crises over the last week to be in any shape to deal with this.

There was a sudden noise from the hall. A key turned briskly in the lock of my front door and Yasmina's voice called out brightly: 'Oh, Matilda. Are you there? I've left my purse behind!'

We were all caught by surprise, but Edward got over it first. While I was still registering a varied gamut of slow-motion feelings, he launched himself out of his chair and made a grab for the gun. I think I may have screamed a warning. They were both tall, but Byron T. was beefy where Edward was lean, and young where Edward was, regrettably, old. They struggled, locked together, grunting. You didn't need second sight to see that Edward didn't have a snowball's chance in hell.

I never thought I'd have the brass to hit someone

183

on the head with a bottle. It's the thought of the skull cracking that puts me off. But I have to say, today it just came naturally. I seized the bottle of red wine that was standing ready on the draining board, and bashed Byron T. over the head with it as if I'd been doing it all my life. The bottle shattered, and glass and wine went everywhere, all over the three of us. Edward disengaged abruptly and stood back, spluttering. Byron T. gave a sort of strangled grunt, sagged at the knees and fell, the Colossus of Rhode Island, to the floor. The gun dropped from his hand and as Edward bent unthinkingly, I yelled at the top of my voice: 'Don't pick it up!' He froze in the act, bent double. Yasmina appeared in the doorway, her face a picture of amazement.

I wish I'd had a camera.

Chapter 24

Fortunately for me, Byron T. had a thick skull. The police arrived before he came round, and he was taken off in a *panier à salade*, very silent, in handcuffs. Inspector Guillaume was the nearest I'd ever seen him to happy. He wasn't exactly smiling, but he looked a lot less miserable than usual. Policemen like finding the murder weapon. It makes them feel secure.

Byron T. had fooled us all very cleverly. His hired car had been quietly parked in my street for the past ten days, together with his hired mobile phone and, presumably, the gun. He'd got himself a separate room on the grounds of Edward's snoring, and his supposed allergy to cats had been a simple device to make sure his door was always kept closed without arousing our suspicion. The police experts were divided in their minds as to whether he was sane or as mad as the proverbial hatter, and decided to get an American psychologist over in case they were missing something cultural.

The police picked up Monique Ryckmans in Rio before she'd even had time to unpack her bikini, and put her on the next plane back. She wouldn't be seeing the outside of a prison cell for quite some time. The Andrieu empire was in shreds. Half a dozen employees were arrested, including Monsieur Paul. A Belgian Moriarty, I'd said jokingly. Not only had he been the one who'd locked me in the store-room, but he'd been driving the lorry that nearly killed Edward outside my front door. Anny Baeke turned out to be innocent of everything except unrequited love. And monkey-tricks, of course. But losing the object of her desire was sufficient punishment. It was too bad that he happened also to be the object of mine.

Guillaume followed my advice and tipped off the animal lobby, but only a couple of minor resignations resulted in Belgium, while further afield a few small diplomatic heads rolled and a number of shady characters went underground for a month or two. But the Andrieu network was well and truly smashed, and the whole thing got a high profile in the international press – always useful because it makes governments clean up their acts, for a while at least.

The Andrieu businesses were rolled up, of course. But an environmental agency took over Les Fauves, and a Swedish group made a bid for the Burgundia almost as soon as the For Sale sign went up, and no doubt made a killing, if you'll excuse the expression.

Edward and I visited Ilse in hospital and found her much restored, partly by Guillaume's assurance that no action would be taken against her, and partly because of the bracing presence of her mother, a small, no-nonsense lady with a determined manner. She was taking Ilse back to Germany for a holiday in the Black Forest and after that, they would see. I got the feeling that Ilse was going to be taken in hand, which was probably just what she needed.

Edward, in an orgy of remorse and self-flagellation, wrote to the authorities concerned with the naming of bugs, and got his particular bug rechristened.

'*Gryllulus haycastellani-hendersoni*. How does that sound?'

'Terrible,' I replied. 'Can't you shorten it?'

'No,' he said irritably.

'Well, just call it *Gryllulus hendersoni*. After all, she did discover it.'

'She found it. I discovered it,' he said with dignity.

Hortense showed what she thought of this argument by jumping on the table and parking her rear-end on the letter he was writing. Edward put his pen down and began to stroke her ears.

'What happened to your Wolfman?' he asked, glancing at me shrewdly over Hortense's head.

'Gone to Italy,' I said shortly.

'Just as well. He wouldn't have stood the pace. He'll marry some nice girl and they'll raise wolf-cubs together. Ah, the patter of tiny lupine feet. Incidentally, your lawyer fancies you.'

'No, he doesn't,' I said, startled.

Edward grinned in the annoying way people have when they think they know something you don't.

Richard Grandville had been his usual diffident self when we had met last. We had shaken hands, rather self-consciously, and no mention had been made of meeting again. But come to think of it, his bill had been remarkably modest under the circumstances.

'So what's next?' Edward asked. Hortense, eyes closed, was in an ecstatic trance. 'Work,' I said, making a face. 'No money, no eat. And it might be nice to lead a normal life for a month or two.'

'Ah. That's a pity,' Edward said. 'What about Alaska?'

'What about it?'

'The last great wilderness on earth. I'm going there next month and I need an assistant. I thought you might like to come. We make a good team.'

I began to laugh. 'I've done enough bottle-washing in my time. Advertise for a popsy.'

Edward put on an expression of deep outrage.

187

'That's no way to talk to your father,' he said. And then he added: 'I know thirty-six years is a long time to catch up on, but we could make a start.'

Well, after all, who needs work?